"I guess I'm not th
of a train wreck." ~~Mandy reached up and~~
ran her fingers through Jarrod's hair.

The simple action made his breath catch in his throat. He'd forgotten how good it felt to have someone's fingers twist in his hair.

"Jarrod, I want you to know that I'm grateful—for everything. You've done so much for me and Anya. And I promise, no matter what happens, just as you have saved us from getting hurt, I will do my best to keep from hurting you."

Just when he had thought he couldn't feel any more at odds with himself, she had to go and say something so tremendously sweet, and soul crushing.

A flood of thoughts of morality and desire moved through him, and in its wake were dreams of what could be.

He stood up and wrapped her in his arms. This woman, this beautiful person, could be his future. She could be his everything.

He pressed his lips against hers.

Acknowledgments

This series wouldn't have been possible without a great team of people, including Melanie Calahan and Clare Wood, my #1k1hr friends, Jill Marsal and the editors at Harlequin—thank you for all your hard work.

Also, thank you to my readers. You keep me writing.

IN HIS SIGHTS

DANICA WINTERS

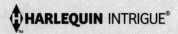

To Mac.

Thanks for always believing in me.

ISBN-13: 978-1-335-13626-8

In His Sights

Copyright © 2019 by Danica Winters

Recycling programs for this product may not exist in your area.

This edition published by arrangement with Harlequin Books S.A.

For questions and comments about the quality of this book, please contact us at CustomerService@Harlequin.com.

Printed in U.S.A.

www.Harlequin.com

Danica Winters is a multiple-award-winning, bestselling author who writes books that grip readers with their ability to drive emotion through suspense and occasionally a touch of magic. When she's not working, she can be found in the wilds of Montana, testing her patience while she tries to hone her skills at various crafts—quilting, pottery and painting are not her areas of expertise. She believes the cup is neither half-full nor half-empty, but it better be filled with wine. Visit her website at danicawinters.net.

Books by Danica Winters

Harlequin Intrigue

Stealth

Hidden Truth
In His Sights

Mystery Christmas

Ms. Calculation
Mr. Serious
Mr. Taken

Smoke and Ashes
Dust Up with the Detective
Wild Montana

Visit the Author Profile page at Harlequin.com.

CAST OF CHARACTERS

Jarrod Martin—The head of STEALTH and the Martin family, he chooses to take on one more mission and contracts out with the CIA on an investigation into H&K and their possible ties with nefarious antigovernment groups. But this mission turns out to be far more than he bargained for when he meets the beautiful, smart and sexy Mindy.

Mindy Kohl—A socialite with a backbone and nerves of steel, Mindy is done being told what she can and can't do—especially when her brother, Daniel, goes missing and she is forced to work with Jarrod Martin to learn the truth.

Anya Jeffery—Mindy's sweet and precocious five-year-old niece with Down syndrome. She was ill-treated by her mother and under the care of a nanny who may not have her best interests at heart.

Daniel Jeffery—Mindy's half brother and CEO of H&K Gun Manufacturing. He may be investing large sums of money in foreign governments who, inexplicably, are making huge strides in weapons development and implementation, to the detriment of the US government as well as allied forces.

Hans Anders—Member of the Riksdag and the man standing in the way of H&K opening a new manufacturing plant in Sweden.

STEALTH—The Martins' private government contracting company, known for taking down those deemed unsavory by the US government and its citizens.

Bill Arthur—The questionable-at-best CIA rookie with secrets in his heart.

Chad Martin—Jarrod's brother and the family clown. He takes very little seriously, but he is the man in the shadows who often controls far more than anyone expects.

Trish Martin—The Martins' youngest sibling. He was killed in action in Turkey while STEALTH was running an undercover operation in which they infiltrated terrorist organizations through the illicit gun trade.

Fenrisulfr Bayural—The leader of the Bozkurtlar, or the Gray Wolves, a terrorist organization that works around the globe and leaves only murder and mayhem in their wake.

Riksdag—The highest decision-making assembly in Sweden, members of which may or may not be as crooked as they are dangerous.

Chapter One

It was impossible to change a person. However, it was possible to change a person's opinion—given the right motivation. And, as it so happened, death was one hell of a motivator.

Jarrod Martin looked at the man strapped to the chair in the center of the interrogation room, deep in the guts of Camp Four within the confines of Camp Delta, also known as Guantanamo Bay or Gitmo. The air was hot, reminding him of his days in Iraq, but heavy with the dank humidity and the scent of sweat and fear.

As soon as he was done here he could make his way back out into the world…a world that didn't out-wardly appear to be at war. And yet, no matter where he was in the world or under what regime, there was always some unspoken or unacknowledged war— even at his new home in Montana, and it was one of the many reasons he was in no rush to head there.

For the good of the people and for himself,

he was here—the man sent in to rectify security threats and take down terrorists.

"Cut him loose," he ordered, looking to the two agents he had been given as guards.

"Sir, this man is a known criminal," the agent nearest him said. He looked to be about twenty-five, and Jarrod swore he could even see a smear of milk on his upper lip.

He held back a chuckle. "What's your name?"

"Agent Arthur," the man said.

"Well, Agent Arthur, I didn't ask for your opinion." The last thing he wanted, or needed, was someone questioning how he did his job. He'd been involved in interrogations long enough to know what did and didn't work—and he didn't need some know-it-all rookie his boss had stuck him with rocking the boat.

"My apologies, sir," the man said, walking over to their suspect and unlocking his restraints. "I just thought—"

Jarrod shot him a look that said *shut up* in every language. "His feet, as well," Jarrod said, motioning in the direction of the shackles.

The rookie zipped his lip and set to work. Jarrod took one more look over his suspect's file, for effect rather than the need to know. He'd seen more than his fair share of these kinds of guys—the corporate jerks who thought they were above the law…right until they found themselves sitting in his interrogation chair.

Daniel Jeffery, the young CEO of Heinrich and Kohl gun manufacturing, sat back in his chair and looked around the room. He looked like a wolf that had just been set loose from a snare. Jarrod held back a mirth-filled smile. Given enough time, he would turn this wolf into a pup who would beg to do his bidding.

"How are you doing, Daniel? Do you need anything? Water? Sandwich?" he asked, trying to ingratiate himself with the man.

Daniel brushed off the legs of his dress pants, attempting to rid himself of the detritus of captivity. "I could use a latte and a fresh set of clothes," he said. "I don't know why you think it was okay to bring me here. I've done nothing wrong."

Sure, he could argue all he wanted. But if he was innocent, the CIA would have never called STEALTH, Jarrod's independent military contractor team and the CIA's harbinger of dirty work. He and his team were like the Ghostbusters of bad guys—the government always called them in when they'd run out of legal ways to handle those who needed to be dealt with.

In fact, it had been a running joke among his brothers and sisters to the point that he had programmed his phone to notify him with the *Ghostbusters* theme song whenever they messaged him. And back at home, after a few rounds of whiskey, their nights always devolved into poor renditions of eighties hit songs.

The thought of his family made his core clench. He needed to be with them, especially after the death of their sister Trish, but he couldn't bring himself to face them…not yet. For now it was so much easier to stare down corrupt businessmen, killers and thieves. They were people he could understand.

Jarrod motioned to the other guard. "Would you please run and get Mr. Jeffery a coffee?" He turned to his detainee. "You take cream and sugar?"

The man shook his head.

"Great," Jarrod said, glancing back to the guard. "And grab him a pair of Gitmo's finest. I'm feeling like a tan jumpsuit would be a good fit. It's not quite as nice as the suit Mr. Jeffery has there, but it will get the job done."

The agent gave him a tight nod and left the room as the detainee started to argue. Agent Arthur stepped closer to the man but stopped when Jarrod shot him a look.

Jarrod could remember the days when he had been a young, dumb newbie, just waiting to jump in and take control in every situation. Thankfully, he'd had his father to show him the ropes in STEALTH—and the man, though he had his fair share of faults, had been as patient as a saint.

In moments like these, he reminded himself of his father's words: *The only thing you can do well without thinking is falling in love. The rest of the time you got to shut your mouth and pay attention.*

"Now, Mr. Jeffery, do you know why you are here today?" he asked, taking a chair from the corner and moving it directly in front of his detainee.

"All I know is that I was visiting our company's office in Washington, DC, when you and a bunch of fed clowns thought it was okay to come in and take me down like I was some kind of goddamned mob boss." Daniel pointed at Jarrod, his actions aggressive and angry. He would need to calm the man down.

"I'm sorry you feel like it was an invasion of your professional life," Jarrod said, trying to empathize. "I know you're the boss and under a lot of public scrutiny." He held Daniel's eye. "It's my goal to get you back home as quickly as I can. I'm your advocate. And perhaps we can even make this all work in your favor."

The man sat in silence for a moment. "I appreciate that." He stared daggers at Agent Arthur, who stood in the corner.

"Absolutely," Jarrod said, even though he was struggling to keep his personal judgment of the man at bay. "So, according to what I've been told about your case, they believe you may have been selling state secrets to foreign governments—

North Korea, to be exact. Is there any merit to their claims?" he said, careful to distance himself from the authorities.

Daniel gave him a look of complete disbelief. He opened his mouth and shut it a few times before finally speaking. "I...I don't know about any of that. And I sure as hell didn't sell anything to North Korea." Strangely, his gaze kept slipping to Agent Arthur as though he feared the man.

"If that is the truth, then I think everything should go well here today." Jarrod sat down in the chair across from Daniel. He put his knee between the man's knees, just close enough to be inside of his personal space, but not so close as to make him clam up.

"So, you believe me?" Daniel asked.

He didn't believe the guy any further than he could throw him, but he wasn't there to be judge and jury—he was only there to find out exactly what this detainee knew. "Unless you give me a reason to mistrust you, I think we can be friends. I believe in the American system of justice— innocent until proven guilty."

In reality, almost everyone who worked in law enforcement felt exactly the opposite. Everyone was guilty of something. Maybe not for the crime they were investigating, but there wasn't a single soul out there who wasn't guilty of some wrongdoing—and it was his job to find out exactly what.

The man let out a long exhale. "But what about him?" He paused, pointing in the direction of Arthur with his chin. "I wish I knew what you are doing here." There was an odd strangled sound to Daniel's tone.

"Don't worry about him," Jarrod said, waving him off.

"How do you work with all these meatheads and not lose your mind?"

Jarrod chuckled. "I know you met us on a crap day, but some of them aren't so bad. I'm sure you've got employees at Heinrich and Kohl who are about the same way—duller than a butter knife."

The man laughed, loosening up. "You know it. There are days where I swear some of my employees ate paint chips as kids."

Good, he was establishing camaraderie.

"Any of those employees at H&K got it out for you?"

The man shrugged, staring down at the floor. "If you're a giraffe, there's always going to be hyenas nipping at your ankles."

"You think any of these hyenas could be behind this leak?"

Agent Arthur shuffled his feet like he was growing bored with the interrogation. No doubt, he wanted to handle it differently, but Jarrod didn't care. What he really wanted to do was send the rookie out, but the CIA had made it clear that he needed a guard with him at all times. They should've known by now that he could take care of himself, and yet that kind of hubris made him more like the rookie Arthur than he cared to admit.

Daniel looked over at the offending agent and then back to him, weighing them both in a glance. "There's always someone gunning for me. I'm sure that whatever it is you think I did, it was done by someone else. I have no interest in implicating myself in some political nonsense. I already have more than enough to keep me busy."

"You're not hurting for money or resources?" Jarrod asked.

"No, I make a really good salary. Our stocks are running high, and the long-term forecast looks great."

Though the man was nearly the picture of innocence, Jarrod didn't buy everything Daniel was saying. The CIA wouldn't have brought him here if Daniel didn't have some strong motivation to sell secrets about his weaponry and government contracts.

"Let's go back to this idea of your hyenas," Jarrod said. "Is there anyone you suspect might have set you up?"

Daniel looked torn, like there was something he wanted to say. He looked at Agent Arthur and then back to Jarrod. "For starters…" He stood up.

Agent Arthur took a step toward him, the action unnecessarily aggressive. "You need to sit down," Agent Arthur ordered.

Daniel ignored the man, instead reaching in his pocket.

"Get your hands out of your pockets, now!" Agent Arthur roared.

"Agent, take a step back," Jarrod said, trying to regain control. They didn't need this getting out of hand when they were just starting to get somewhere.

Daniel pulled what looked like a pen from his pocket. As he moved, a picture fell down, drifting to the floor. The team must have frisked the man, and he had gone through a metal detector.

"Where did you get—" Jarrod started.

"Put down the weapon!" Agent Arthur yelled, pulling his gun and pointing it straight at the man's center mass.

If Jarrod hadn't been shocked, it would have made him laugh to have the agent call a pen a weapon.

Daniel clicked the pen, and as he did, a shot rang out. The percussive blast roared through the room, momentarily deafening him. Instinctively, Jarrod's hand went to his gun.

Daniel crumpled to his knees and dropped the pen. His hands moved to his chest. Blood seeped from a tiny hole directly over his heart. He looked at Arthur, then down at his hands. Blood collected at the creases of his fingers and dripped downward. "Arthur, you two-faced bastard."

"What in the hell did you do, Agent? It was a goddamned pen!" He rushed to Daniel's side just as he slumped to the ground.

"He was drawing a weapon. I thought he was a threat," Agent Arthur said, waving his hand at the offending man like his choice to shoot was obvious. "My actions were completely justified."

Applying pressure, Jarrod tried to stop the bleeding even though he knew his efforts were in vain. The blood soaked through the man's clothing and spread over the ground, wetting Jarrod's knees. So much blood.

He looked to the pen. There was something off about it, and as he picked it up, he noticed that it had a tiny pill-like plastic piece filled with powder instead of a nib. He could only guess what was inside, but he wouldn't have been surprised if it had been cyanide.

Beside the pen was a picture of a young woman. She had long brown hair and a playful, confident smile. He flipped the photo over with the tip of his fingernail, careful not to disturb the evidence. On the back it read: "She will be next."

This time, death had won, but if he acted fast, and found the woman in the picture, perhaps he could stop another person from falling victim to life's fickle master.

Chapter Two

She hated this, being stuck in yet another stupid meeting. Sometimes she could have sworn her job was to do nothing more than listen to the mindless ramblings of the H&K board and their endless stream of guests.

Mindy Kohl looked down at her watch, trying to subtly check the time without making the members of the Swedish parliament, the Riksdag, think she was being rude. She had to follow the rules of etiquette or risk offending the leaders who would determine the fate of her company's expansion, but it didn't make her any less squirmy.

She hated this job. Pandering was best left to those who enjoyed the thrill of the hunt and the glory that came from winning. It was really no wonder her half brother had loved it, right up until he had become CEO of Heinrich and Kohl. Even in his new role, he'd still hovered, constantly reminding her that she was to do her best, as they had much to lose.

Then again, not everything was terrible about her new position: it afforded her a great deal of travel and leisure—though this time she got to stay home in the heart of NYC. She was relieved that after this brutally long and drawn-out meeting, she could go home.

There was a man standing to her left beside the table. His name badge said Jarrod Martin. She didn't recognize the man, but he appeared to be in his early thirties and comprised entirely of muscle. He'd come in with the entourage that accompanied the parliament members, and was likely acting as a guard. But, instead of bringing her comfort, every time she looked at him, she felt an unwelcome warmth cascade through her.

If only it were a year ago, when her life had been focused on nothing more than giving in to the whims of her heart, she would have easily made the man her lover. She caught herself glancing down, hoping to see if his back was as scrumptious as his front. She wasn't disappointed.

Her contact, and lead ambassador for the Riksdag, Hans Anders, cleared his throat as he took the floor. He was sitting three down from her at the conference table. His fingers were tented in front of him as he spoke, a look of distaste forming when he addressed Mindy directly. He clearly thought a woman in gun manufacturing was some kind of farce. She'd always thought that the Swedish were more progressive when it came to empowering women, but clearly there were some men in every culture who thought it best for a woman to stay in the kitchen.

Needless to say, she hated the bastard.

"Furthermore," Hans continued, "it is not in our best interest to allow a machining plant in our countryside. While we welcome international businesses with open arms, by bringing in a gun manufacturer, it could be misconstrued as our implied consent and role in the international gunrunning trade."

"Sir, while I appreciate your thoughts and hear what you are saying, I humbly disagree," she said, forcing herself to remain seated even though all she wanted to do was stand, face him down and put an end to this argument. "My company is in no way an advocate for international violence. We pride ourselves on our stellar record within the global market. While we cannot control where or how our guns are used, the same can be said about many other incredibly lucrative businesses—such as pharmaceuticals. Would you deny a person access to a lifesaving medication because you are afraid of the medication being misused?"

Hans opened his mouth, no doubt wishing to rebut, but she didn't give him the chance to speak. She had the floor, and no matter what some man thought, she was going to keep it.

"What you are talking about is a what-if, while you—and the entire Riksdag—should be focused on the bottom line of our proposal. This year alone, our plants in the United States have brought in $7.2 billion in taxable income. We believe, should you allow us to open our plant, we will either match or exceed this figure every year for your country."

Hans looked as though he had swallowed a sour grape. Money always took precedence. Really, this endeavor would be a win-win for both parties. All she had to do was prove it.

"Why don't we take a little break, and we can come back and discuss this further after lunch." Hans stood up and shuffled through the papers of her proposal.

Though Hans wasn't the head of the parliament, he sure acted like it. Without his approval, this would go nowhere. She'd spend the next six months apologizing to her brother and the board, and trying to find a suitable replacement for the warehouse and manufacturing building they had purchased in Sweden.

"That sounds wonderful," she said. "And please note, my family's company always strives to create a healthy environment for employees. It would be an honor to have our company located in a place that has an empowered and ambitious workforce."

Smiles appeared on the faces of the men and women around the table.

Maybe she wasn't so bad at pandering after all.

The guard to her left, Jarrod, stepped closer to her. "If you'd like, I'd love to escort you to lunch. I hear there's a great deli just around the corner."

Her mouth watered, but she wasn't sure if it was because of the man who'd asked her or the prospect of salty, fatty meats. Either way, she was happy to oblige. "Of course, though I thought you were with the parliament members." She motioned to the group around them.

He smiled. "I doubt anyone will miss me. As it is, I was brought here just to be a visible presence in the meeting room."

"Oh yeah? Did they think that I was the kind of woman who would jump on the table and threaten them if I didn't get what I wanted?" She stood up and made a show of her petite, but heavyset frame. "I'm hardly equipped—or likely—to throw my weight around."

"I've always found that one shouldn't underestimate the power of an angry woman." He laughed.

"If you don't feed me soon, you'll get to see exactly how hangry I can get," she teased.

"Well, I'm only going with you if you promise not to take me down," he said with a laugh.

A wave of torrid thoughts washed through her mind. She couldn't help the heat that rose in her body and colored her cheeks.

She tried to cap all of her dirty thoughts, but

it was a losing battle. She hadn't had sex in six months. A girl only had so much willpower.

Maybe she could just take him during their lunch break. They had an hour, and with the way she was feeling, that would leave them plenty of time to cuddle afterward.

Oh goodness, what was wrong with her?

Maybe going with him to lunch wasn't such a great idea after all. If things were going to devolve into some midday rendezvous, she was probably better off staying in her office.

Whenever her body took the lead, it never seemed to end well.

When she had been younger, to say she had been a bit of a party girl was an understatement. Until her father's death, she had been spending her time—and her father's money—shopping, traveling, hanging out with her friends…and having her heart broken by men.

Throughout the years, people had told her she was spoiled. However, she had never really seen it that way. Though she had been economically gifted, it came at a price. Her mother had died when she was young and her father's success had taken its toll. During his rare appearances at home, he had spent all of his time in his office yelling at hapless underlings or business associates. He rarely had actual free time, but when he did he liked to spend those days on the golf course.

Mindy didn't blame him for his parental failings. However, she was extremely tired of having to justify how she had become such a headstrong and wild woman—she couldn't have been anything else, thanks to her free-range childhood.

She allowed the members of the Swedish parliament to exit in front of her in a gesture of goodwill. Jarrod stayed by her side. His arm brushed against hers, making the hairs on her skin stand at attention. It was as though there were a charge between them, something resembling static electricity, but she tried not to pay it any mind. Maybe it was nothing more than her thousand-dollar shoes scuffing against the carpet. It struck her as funny that even now, after all of her dalliances with men, it was still possible to mistake attraction for actual electricity.

That was what it was—her attraction to him was science. They were like two magnets drawn to each other by nature's cosmic forces—nothing more. But dang, those forces felt good.

She waited for a few moments, until they were alone in the room, and then she turned to Jarrod. "Look, if you have a job to do, we can always meet after work." It came out sounding far more lurid than she had actually wanted it to. Rather, she had hoped it would be an invitation for a real, grown-up date…one that wouldn't resemble anything like the Netflix-and-chill dates of her past.

He gave her a melting smile. She got the impression that a real smile was something he didn't experience often. "I appreciate the offer, but I'm here for your protection." There was something in the way that he spoke, like each beat was measured and well thought out, which made her wonder if there was something he wasn't telling her.

"I don't believe I'll need a bodyguard with a bunch of old Swedes."

Jarrod's smile widened, but a veil of mystery moved over his eyes. "I don't believe that was quite it." He helped her with her jacket, slipping it over her shoulders, and then he handed over her purse and phone.

It wasn't particularly cold outside, but fall in New York was a mercurial thing. One minute it could be sunny and seventy, and the next snow would be floating from the sky with a nor'easter on its heels.

They rode down in the elevator, sandwiched between strangers and so close that she could feel his breath against the back of her neck. Their bodies touched as she was pressed farther into the elevator with each descending floor. Heat radiated from him, and she tried to stop herself from moving any closer. They were already treading on dangerous ground.

It seemed to take forever to get to the lobby, and she counted her breaths in an attempt to think about anything besides the painfully handsome man behind her. If she closed her eyes, she could make out the shapely contoured goatee and the slight curve of his lips. Oh, those lips. She could kiss those lips.

She shifted her weight from one foot to the other, and once again brushed him—making a fire course up from where their bodies had touched, burning into her cheeks.

When the elevator doors opened, she nearly sprinted out—it was her only chance of escaping. Yet, as soon as she reached the glass doors at the front of the building, she turned around and waited for him.

She could control herself. If nothing else, this was a test. If she could refrain from jumping his bones, she had made significant strides in her personal development. If not, well… She'd have a little more work to do when it came to her boundaries.

"You okay?" he asked, finally catching up to her.

She nodded. "Absolutely, though I have to admit I have a hard time in such enclosed spaces."

He gave her an odd look, like he was deciding whether or not he should believe her. "From the meeting, it seems as though Hans has something against you. What did you do to the poor guy?"

She was thankful he was changing the subject. "Actually, Hans has always had a thing against my family. My father purchased a building and started developing it for H&K's expansion some five years ago. Hans has been blocking our move into their country ever since. We've finally reached a place in our growth where we're going to have to do something or start looking at other countries. Unfortunately, our father invested a large sum of money into the development of this plan and if we walk away now, we'd lose all of the time and money that has gone into it."

Jarrod gave a thoughtful nod. "Did your father ever let you in on why Hans didn't want you there?"

She shook her head as they walked out into the New York air. She both loved and hated the way the city smelled of people—sweat and body odor—cars and industry. In many ways, she didn't miss this city when she spent time at H&K's DC offices.

Though she hadn't talked to him in a couple of days, Daniel was probably chomping at the bit to learn how this meeting had gone. They had a lot riding on this deal and it was her first run of this kind. Just the thought of letting him down made her stomach ache.

Ahead of them in the mash of people was Hans. His bald head looked like something on a bobble-head doll, bouncing as the man walked among his guards and the other members of the parliament.

Her heels clicked on the concrete and they stopped at the crosswalk. "From what I know about Hans," she said, motioning in the direction of the devil in question, "he had a distaste for my father. I think it had something to do with a former business deal gone bad. Something in the nineties. My father never went into great detail, but it's abundantly clear that Hans is the kind of man who can carry a decades-long familial grudge."

"I know all about those," he said.

"Where are you from?" she asked.

He looked at her for a moment, like he was deciding if he wanted to answer. Or maybe it was more about how much he wanted to reveal to her—she couldn't be sure.

"My family is from here, the Bronx, actually. However, we just moved to Montana. I'm here finishing up some last-minute things before heading west."

"Montana?" She'd heard wonderful things about the state and its picturesque scenery and wildlife. "Aren't you afraid of the bears?"

"Once again, I find angry women far more terrifying."

"That sounds like it comes from some dark and horrific place. I'm going to need to hear that story," she said, giving him a teasing smile.

"I wish I were kidding, but I have a faint bite mark from one of the women I had to guard. It's just above my knee," he said, lifting his leg like she could see the mark beneath his dress pants. "I swear it gets sore to the touch before any major storms."

"That is the most ridiculous thing I have ever heard. And I would hate to ask what the woman was doing that had her at knee height." As she spoke, he seemed to gain a bit of color.

The crowd shuffled and they were pushed nearer to Hans, who was standing precariously close to the passing New York traffic.

"Sir," Mindy said, tapping Hans on the arm, "you may want to take a step back. Cabs pull right up to this curb."

Hans gave her a look like she had murdered his first grandchild. "Are you kidding me?" he asked, his voice flecked with his Swedish accent. "First you think you can tell me what I should do with my power inside the parliament, and now you even wish to dictate how I cross the street? You Americans think you know everything."

As the last words fell from his lips, there was the screech of tires and a man's yelling. The sound was strangled, some foreign tongue that Mindy didn't recognize. But even not knowing exactly what the man was saying she could tell by the look on Hans's face that it wasn't good. As the car grew closer, something pitched out of the window. From where she stood, it looked like an envelope. As it hit the ground a plume of white powder erupted into the air. Jarrod grabbed her and threw her to the ground, covering her with his body.

She couldn't breathe, but she wasn't sure whether it was because of his weight or how he had pinned her. As she struggled, her throat burned and her eyes began to water. She tried to push Jarrod off out of some instinctual need to survive. After what seemed like an excruciating amount of time, he rolled off her. As she took a breath, her lungs burned.

He looked as she felt. Tears were streaming down his face and there were dabs of saliva at the corners of his mouth and goatee. She glanced around, a few paces away from them, where Hans was lying on the ground. He was coughing, his body in a fetal position. When he rolled over, she could see that his eyes were swollen shut and blisters had erupted on the skin of his eyelids. There was blood dripping from his face and mouth.

Hans moved as though he was looking at her, even though he couldn't possibly have been able to see her. And then she heard the scream, her scream. Hans reached out in her direction, but she didn't move. She couldn't.

Though she knew she should act and help the man, she feared moving any closer to him. Hans rolled on the ground, his body convulsing.

Whatever the man in the car had thrown at them, it must have been some sort of poison.

Reaching into her purse, she grabbed a wet wipe. It would probably do nothing to help, but she couldn't simply watch Jarrod deteriorate like Hans.

Jarrod took the wipe from her and cleaned his face. "Thank you." He looked dazed, but he got to his feet, tugging her up with him. "We have to get out of here. Now. You're not safe."

From what she could see around her, no one was safe.

She grabbed her phone, dialed 911 and threw the device to the ground in hopes that it would be traced—she could get another phone, they were a dime a dozen.

Jarrod took her hand and pulled her away from the area. She wanted to stay to help, but Jarrod was right. The safest place for them right now was as far away as they could possibly get from the effects of the powder while they waited for EMTs to arrive. For once, she didn't just have herself to think about... Now, she also had Jarrod.

Chapter Three

It had been a long and painful night stuck in the confines of Mount Sinai Beth Israel Hospital. The place was constantly in motion, just like the rest of New York City. It reminded him entirely too much of Camp Delta. Every time he tried to close his eyes after the nerve agent attack, he found himself thinking of all the lives that had been extinguished around him just within the last month. First Trish, then Daniel, and now Hans—everywhere he went, it seemed as though he left corpses in his wake.

Throughout the night, he had made his way down the hall and to Mindy's room to check and make sure she was doing better. For the most part, she had seemed only mildly phased by the chemical attack, but the EMTs had been adamant about bringing them in for all kinds of testing. Luckily, aside from some irritation in his lungs, he had been given the all clear—a far cry from what had happened to Hans, who had died almost instantly on scene. They had taken his body to the morgue, where he was being kept in isolation until they could determine the chemical that had been used in the attack.

He ran his hand down his face and sat up from his hospital bed. Somewhere down the hall he could make out the shrill beeps of an IV pump that had run dry, the monotonous trill of an EKG machine, and the thump and whoosh of a ventilator. The whole place stank of the terror of the long-ill and bedside commodes.

He couldn't stand being in this place another minute. It was worse than being a prisoner of war. At least there, he would have felt he had better odds of making it out alive.

He went to the closet and opened up the melamine door. His clothes were MIA, but there was a small white plastic bag with Beth Israel printed on the side. It contained his wallet and small personal belongings.

He should have expected as much. Of course, they would have disposed of anything that could have been contaminated. He was just fortunate that the hospital staff had stopped using full-blown bodysuits—ones that looked like something straight out of a nuclear war zone—every time they had come in to check on his status.

Thankfully, they hadn't been forced to remain in isolation for long once it was established that the nerve agent used had already dealkylated and run through its half-life. Leaving nothing to chance, he'd already made sure to have the hospital staff send a sample off to his people within the CIA.

A draft worked its way through the back of his gown. It was going to be a breezy walk.

Unlike him, Mindy had seemed to welcome the reprieve from her daily life. She had barely woken once since they had been brought here, possibly an effect of the sedative they had received. His dose had worn off rather quickly, but it had left behind lethargy.

All night he had been thinking about who could have pulled this off and why. He'd come up with many options—ranging from the Swedish government itself all the way to his enemies within the Gray Wolves, a crime syndicate responsible for his sister Trish's death in Turkey.

The Gray Wolves hadn't been exactly quiet about their distaste for Jarrod and his family—and their leader, Bayural, had left them with a warning that he would soon be coming for the entire Martin family. Jarrod had no doubt that the man would come through on his word.

Still, the attack wasn't typical of something the Gray Wolves would have put together. They were far more crass and deliberate. They certainly weren't the type who would hit and run; rather they would face him down as they drew their weapons.

Bayural wanted him and his family to know exactly who was pulling the trigger and why.

So, in essence, he had been left with no real answers—only more questions.

He tied the back of his gown as tightly as he could and made his way down the hall one more time to Mindy's room. Nurses rushed from one room to the next.

At the nurses station stood a man who appeared to be visiting the floor. Jarrod guessed he was in his midthirties, with a high and tight haircut and a stiff back. As Jarrod approached, he made sure to walk closer to the wall, masked by the comings and goings of the staff and visitors, and outside of the man's direct line of sight. Something about him felt off, but he couldn't attribute that feeing to anything obvious about the man's appearance.

Jarrod passed behind him just as the man said something to the nurse at the counter.

Had the people responsible for the nerve agent attack found them? They had to have known they would end up at a hospital.

To be safe, he and Mindy had to get out of there, but at the same time, he didn't want to alarm her. She'd had enough happen in the last twenty-four hours. If she caught a whiff of their being under further attack she might bolt—and likely end up dead.

He tapped on the closed door of her room, and

the TV inside the room clicked off. "Come on in," she said.

His body clenched at the sound of her voice. He had known she would be fine, but there was still a tremendous amount of relief in hearing her sound so healthy.

He looked toward the nurses station one more time, but the suspicious man had turned and was now walking down the hall in the direction of Jarrod's room. He opened her door and slipped inside. He was probably making something out of nothing.

"Hey." He walked over to the window, carefully holding the back of his gown shut.

"Hey." She gave him a look that made him wonder if she was as much at a loss for words as he was.

What could they say about what had happened out there on the street? The nerve agent attack wasn't something a person was forced to endure very often.

For a moment, he considered making a joke about the weather, but he remained silent.

"Feeling okay?" Mindy asked.

He nodded. "You?"

She nodded. "Were you a man of this few words yesterday, too? Or is this something new?"

He cracked a smile. "I have no idea what you're talking about. I'm super chatty."

"Wow, if that's true then you must think I never shut up."

He laughed. "I know for a fact you are quiet sometimes. Last night, for example, you only snored a little bit."

She covered her face with her hands but peeked between her fingers, the action uncomfortably endearing. "You did not come in here when I was sleeping, did you?" she asked, sounding slightly embarrassed that he would have seen her in such a vulnerable state.

"Not in a weird way," he said, trying to make her feel better. "I just wanted to make sure you were doing okay."

She motioned down her body. "As you can see, I made it through unscathed. And I am so ready to get out of here."

"Have you looked in your closet?"

She shook her head. "Why?"

"Well, you and I are going to have matching gowns on the way out. That is, if you want to go AMA with me." He hitched his thumb toward the open door, beckoning her. He tried not to sound hurried or alarmed, but his thoughts kept moving back to the man at the nurses station. If one of them had been the intended target of the nerve agent attack it would be no time at all before the perpetrators found them and finished them off.

"I should've known you were a rebel." She got

up from the bed and walked over to the closet. When she opened the door, there was only a plastic bag filled with her wallet and personal items.

"Crap." She took the bag out and put it on the bed as she rifled through it.

"What?" he asked.

"My phone. It's missing."

"You threw it on the ground, remember?" He could still hear the sound of the glass of the phone crunching as it hit the concrete. He was impressed she had thought to sacrifice her phone for the greater good.

"Dammit… Okay, first stop, I need a new phone." She looked up at him, appearing somewhat frantic at the prospect of being cut off from the outside world.

"If you need to get ahold of someone, like your boyfriend or whatever, you can use my phone." He lifted the bag he was carrying for her to see. "It's in my briefcase." He reached inside his bag and pulled out his cell phone.

He had twenty-seven text messages. Most of them were from his sister Zoey, who had pulled data about the attack and immediately pieced together what had happened. The farther he read down into her texts, the more frantic they had become, with the last unanswered text reading, I'm on my way to NYC if I don't hear back from you. Plane leaves in three hours.

That had been two hours ago.

He tapped out a quick message to let her know that he was okay, but no doubt she would still be beside herself with concern. It was one of the things he loved about his brothers and sisters— or rather, sister…now that Trish was gone.

God, he was never going to get used to that.

He was nowhere near ready to go to Montana and face his family and the ranch without his sister. Though logically he knew it wasn't his fault, he still felt responsible. He was the one who had picked the job. He was the one who had put their family right in the middle of the Gray Wolves crosshairs. If he had just jumped on another ticket and taken another contract instead of this one, they could have been a thousand miles away and unknown to the men who now wanted them dead.

"Everything okay?" Mindy asked, looking at his phone as she walked over to the sink and washed her hands. "Your wife freaking out?"

He couldn't hold back the laugh that escaped him. "No wife. No kids. No home base."

"Ah," she said, drying her hands. "I see. You are the rootless man."

"Is that this generation's way of asking if I'm a playboy?" he asked.

She giggled, the sound melting away even more of his resolve to stay emotionally detached from the beautiful woman standing in front of him with nothing on but a hospital gown. "You aren't that much older than me, are you?"

He wasn't stupid enough or young enough to fall into the trap of asking her exact age, but he guessed she was about twenty-eight. "I'm sure we are within a few years of each other. But I turned in my cool card years ago."

"Clearly," she said, grabbing a clean hospital gown that was folded and sitting beside the sink.

"What are you doing?" he asked.

"You may not care about flashing the outside world, but I need a little more coverage." She indicated her backside.

He laughed. "You and your rear end have nothing to worry about. You have me for coverage."

"Are you saying you want to…cover my rear?" she asked, giving him a disbelieving and yet alluring smile.

He would have been lying if he said no, so he grabbed her bag. "I admit nothing."

"Okay, I see how it is." She took the second gown and slipped it over the first, this time putting the back in the front. "There, now you won't be so tempted…"

Two little hospital gowns and the bedhead she was rocking wouldn't stop the way he was feeling about her. His only option was to get the answers he needed and then get the hell out of Dodge. If he stayed with her too long, he'd have to face his most challenging enemy—his feelings—and as the leader of his family and STEALTH he didn't have time or the freedom for such a mind-set.

He peered out the door of her room and waited for a nurse to turn the corner. "Let's go."

She followed behind as he tried to seem as nonchalant as possible while making their way to the back stairwell.

He held the door open for her, and she started downward. Her footfalls echoed in the concrete stairwell, sounding like spring raindrops clearing away the dusty remnants of his wintery soul.

He took one more glance behind them, but the man from the nurses station was nowhere to be seen.

Yes. He was making something out of nothing. Perhaps the attack had been intended for Hans and they had merely been bystanders.

Regardless, they were lucky to be alive, and it was his mission to keep it that way for as long as it took to get the information he needed about Mindy and her family's role in the stolen government secrets.

At least, that was what he needed to tell himself in order to remain at arm's length from this woman. If he let this get personal, he was going to find himself in trouble. And trouble was one thing already rampant in his life.

"I get that we are leaving AMA and all, but

why are you acting like we're being chased?" she asked, stopping at the entrance to the second floor.

He wanted her to keep moving, so he made his way past her hoping it would urge her along.

"You don't think whoever was behind this attack was coming after me, do you?" she pressed.

Her…him… Hans… He couldn't be sure.

Maybe whoever had pitched the nerve agent was trying to take all three down in one fell swoop.

"Is there a reason you think that may be the case?" he asked, giving nothing away.

She looked away from him, but not before he saw the flicker of concern and fear move across her face.

She held secrets, but he was certain he could get her to loosen her grip and hand them over to him. All he needed was a little more time, a bit more pressure and an increment of fear. Maybe now was the time to talk of murder.

Chapter Four

The Lyft driver hadn't spoken to them, which was just fine by Mindy. She hated the formality and awkwardness that came with forced small talk with a single-serving stranger. It wasn't that she wasn't nice or didn't want to be kind to others; it was just that with everything in her own life, giving any more emotionally—even ten minutes to a stranger—threatened what little control she had left. She was so tired.

As they arrived at her Upper West Side brownstone, Jarrod got out and walked around to her side, opening the car door for her. The gesture was as welcome as it was unexpected. It was a rare New York man who still had manners, or perhaps it was just that the prep-school kind of men she dated had let manners fall by the wayside. Maybe this man could finally bring a bit more civility and old-world charm into her life.

"Thanks," she said, holding her hospital gowns

in place like they were a Givenchy cocktail dress instead of the blue checkered fabric that had been worn by countless others.

She couldn't wait to take a shower. Yet, if she left him alone in her apartment, she would be the one devoid of manners. Assuming that he was coming in. He probably had better places to be, including reporting back to his Swedish bosses.

"You are welcome, ma'am."

Oh no, he didn't… Old-world charm be damned.

"Ma'am? Really?" she asked, raising a brow. "What am I, eighty?"

He laughed, the sound rich and baritone, as strong and virile as the man it belonged to. "I'm sorry, I guess my upbringing is showing. I didn't mean anything by it."

She didn't believe that for a second. Maybe he hadn't meant to call her old, but he had meant to imply that she had the upper hand in whatever social hierarchy lay between them. On one hand, the feminist in her loved the idea of holding the power, but on the other, if they were to become anything more than friends… Well, he didn't seem like the kind of man who would be willing to have the woman in the driver's seat. But he had yet prove he was the man she assumed he was.

She fished in the hospital's plastic bag until she found her keys. "You're fine."

None of what she thought or felt about the man

really even mattered. This was nothing, just a man being chivalrous after a near-death experience. She couldn't project some kind of hero fantasy on him. He barely even seemed interested in her.

"I appreciate you taking time out of your schedule to see me home," she said, unsure whether or not she should ask him in or let him go.

The thought of being alone made her hands shake, and she struggled to put the key into the lock.

"Here, let me help you with that," he said, taking the keys and unlocking the door.

Damn.

She hated being this weak in front of a man like him. Her confidence was her armor, and up until the moment she'd met Jarrod, it had been seemingly impenetrable. Now here she was, so far away from her safe emotional space.

Yep, he had to go.

Still, she hated the thought of being alone.

If she had been the target of the attack, for all she knew, there could be someone waiting just behind these doors. The thought made chills tumble down her spine.

She had to be confident. She had to be strong. She had to let him leave and walk through the door alone. It was the only way she could fall back into her normal life.

"Do you mind if I use your restroom?" he asked.

Ugh. There went her mantra and any measure of self-control she had left. She could hardly let him stand out here on her stoop, but letting him in now wouldn't be just good manners—she would be letting him into her life.

"Go for it," she said, slipping off her Hermès flats, the only piece of clothing the hospital hadn't cut her out of. She pitched them into the garbage pail inside the coat closet.

He watched her with curiosity as she closed the closet door. "You know, your shoes are probably fine to keep. Whatever they used on us, it's worn off by now."

"It's all right," she said with a shrug.

"They looked expensive."

They had been, but it didn't matter. If she kept them she would think of the attack every time she put them on. She would already have to pass by the street corner every time she went to her office. She didn't need any more triggers—at least none beyond the man who stood in front of her.

"It's okay, I have another pair just like them." That wasn't entirely true, but she wasn't ready to completely open up to him. "If you'd like, you are welcome to use the shower upstairs. We can call out and get you some new clothes, as well." She looked him up and down, trying to estimate what size he wore, but a flirtatious expression forced her eyes away.

"If you wouldn't mind, that would be great. You'd save me from going back to my hotel room in a hospital gown. Did you see the way the Lyft driver looked at me when he came to pick us up?" He chuckled.

"We really did look like two escapees, didn't we?" She waved down at her gown. "This is one look that I'm happy to see go. In fact, I may take a shower in my en suite when you take yours."

He raised a brow. "How big is this place?" He stepped into the living room, and his gaze moved to the original Picasso that hung over the mantel.

She'd always loved that piece, a bit of surrealism in a traditional world. In a way it reminded her of herself, a woman working in a man's world. Sure, it wasn't unheard-of to have a woman hold a seat on a board, but a woman at the seat of a gun manufacturer's board was unusual.

She shrugged. "Big enough?" She gave him a half grin in an attempt to downplay her elaborate dwelling.

"Is that a real Picasso?" he asked, pointing at the colorful painting.

She nodded. "He was a friend of the family's in the 1930s. He made it specifically for my great-grandfather, but he never particularly liked it so it sat in storage for years until I took over the place."

Jarrod walked across the room, staring at the

painting. "Beautiful." He looked back at her. "Why don't you have security staff?"

The thought of hiring security had crossed her mind many times, but she rarely spent enough time here to concern herself. She'd have to start looking into changing things. "I'm new to living completely in the public eye and drawing all the scrutiny that comes with it. My father was the former CEO for Heinrich & Kohl. That is, until he passed away last year."

"I'm sorry to hear about your father's death. From what I've heard, he was a good man."

She was surprised that, working for the Swedes, he had heard even a single good word about her father. "So, you know about my family?"

"A little bit, but not much. Just what I could glean from the meetings I've attended."

She wasn't sure if he was trying to be vague or if he really didn't know much about her. Either way, it was strangely endearing. "What do you do for the Riksdag?"

"I don't work for them," he said, all of his attention back on the painting.

"Okay, so who do you work for?" She walked over to her white couch and sat down, arranging her gown to cover her knees.

He turned to her, and his gaze dropped to her hands. She covered her naked ring finger with her other hand, his simple action making her feel almost naked…and vulnerable.

"I work where I'm needed and when I'm called upon."

"That sounds dangerous." And sexy as hell. "If you tell me, would you have to kill me?" she teased, but from the tense look on his face the joke had fallen flat.

He was silent for a moment too long. "Let's just say I'm a man who understands the value in keeping a personal life sacrosanct."

Maybe they had more in common than she had initially thought.

"You're naive if you think that you're safe," he continued.

She felt her hackles rise. "I don't know who you think you are—"

"I didn't mean any offense," he said, raising his hand and motioning her to stop. "I was just saying that I don't think I should leave you here alone. At least not until the NYPD and the FBI get their hands on whoever was behind the attack."

"I'll hire people," she said, trying to gain control over her anger. Whether or not he had meant it, it had still hurt. She didn't need anyone telling her that she was stupid.

"I'm sorry again," he said, sitting down beside her on the couch. "I really didn't mean it like that.

Please forgive me." He looked her straight in the eyes and took her hands in his.

Sweat rose on her skin as she stared into his bottomless blue eyes. She wasn't sure she had ever seen eyes that exact shade before. They reminded her of the color of the deepest ocean, and it seemed that they held just as many mysteries.

But she couldn't forget who she was or change for any man, no matter how handsome. "I don't appreciate being put down. Ever. I know it was unintentional, but don't think that you can talk to me that way."

He looked contrite, bowing his head. "I know. I made a mistake. I just… Well, I don't want to see you get hurt."

What bothered her the most was that he was right in his castigation of her. It had been naive of her to think that she was safe on her own here. She had chosen this place, without a doorman, living a life halfway between obscene wealth and a recent college grad. Her brother had warned her that this day would come, the day when things would change and she would have to start really taking her life and safety into consideration. With a business like theirs, it was only a matter of time until they were on the receiving end of the guns they made. They worked in a volatile business, one full of secrets, underhanded deals and political warfare.

Until now, she had thought they had done a pretty good job of staying out of it.

When it came to dealing with corruption, it was best to walk away—no amount of money was worth dying for.

"I appreciate your apology." She paused, studying his thick, wavy hair. "It's too bad you're working for someone else, or else I'd think about bringing you on as my chief security advisor."

He jerked, looking up at her.

As his gaze pierced through her, she wished she hadn't spoken so fast although she had meant what she said. He would be a valuable asset to her life, especially when it came to her well-being and safety. She wasn't sure that he would be as sound an addition when it came to her heart. Though she was almost certain she could trust him, she wasn't sure she could trust herself.

"I—" he said.

"The shower is upstairs, third door on your left," she said, intentionally interrupting him, fearing what he was about to say.

"Oh, okay," he said, some of the tension leaching from his voice.

"Towels are in the linen closet in the restroom." She motioned toward the stairs, afraid that if she spent one more moment alone with him she would say something else that would bring him even deeper into her life.

He nodded and silently made his way out of the living room and up the stairs. His footfalls echoed on the marble steps, their sad sound cascading down upon her. As the sound quieted, she exhaled long and hard. She needed to get a grip on herself.

She sat down on her couch, picked up her landline telephone and dialed her brother. Daniel's phone went straight to voice mail. "Hey, Danny, I hope everything is going well in DC. Things up here… Well, give me a call when you can." There was a crack in her voice as she spoke. No doubt Daniel would pick right up on it and be worried. "I'm fine, everything is fine, but I hope Anya's okay. Just call."

Ugh.

That wasn't how she had anticipated that going. Once he got her message, she would have to talk him down off a cliff. He'd always been the worrying type. She hung up the phone, half expecting to get a call from him, but nothing came.

She waited for a moment before ascending the stairs to the third floor and to her bedroom. It was just as it had been yesterday, understated but tasteful. She could still pick up the scent of her Mademoiselle perfume as she entered the bathroom.

It was as if nothing had happened.

A towel hung on the hook next to a clean washcloth and bathrobe. The cleaning lady must have come, and all had been replaced and freshened.

In fact, the only thing out of place in the entire house was her.

She pulled off her hospital gowns and tossed them in the bin as she turned on the shower and waited for it to warm. Steam began to rise around her as she stood examining herself in the mirror. For all intents and purposes, she seemed the same. Same eyes, same nose, same cheeks, but nothing felt the same. In one moment everything had changed.

She wasn't entirely sure if it was because of the attack or because of the strange feelings she was experiencing with Jarrod.

It was though she were drawn to him by some invisible force. The words that came out of her mouth even worked to pull him closer. At the same time, all she wanted to do was push him away.

She wrapped a towel around her body and made her way out to her closet. Surveying the racks of clothes, she wasn't sure whether she should go with business attire, or leggings and sweatshirt. Whatever she wore, it would send a message to him, but what she wanted to do was put on comfortable clothes and binge-watch Netflix all day.

She grabbed a pair of jeans and a T-shirt. A happy medium, for them both.

As she reached into her drawer of undergarments, a draft brushed against her bare shoulders.

She started to turn, but a hand wrapped around her neck.

She dropped her clothes. "What in the—"

"Shut up, dammit." A man's hot breath wafted against her skin.

She tried to turn around, but as she struggled, the man's hand tightened. Reaching to her left, she grabbed her Manolo stiletto.

"You can thank your boyfriend for this." His accent was thick, guttural.

"Who are you?"

The tip of a knife pressed into her side. And his hand loosened slightly.

She stole the moment. Raising the shoe, she slammed it down as hard as she could into the man's thigh. She rolled out of his grasp, grabbing her other shoe as he dropped to his knee in pain. He yelled, something in a foreign language she couldn't understand but was sure was a string of expletives.

The man struggled to stand up, limping on his good leg, slashing at her with the knife. She pressed back into her closet as blood poured down the man's leg. She had hit him perfectly in the inner thigh.

"Don't come any closer," she yelled. "Jarrod is coming. He's here. He'll kill you. Jarrod!"

The man lunged at her with the knife. She watched his eyes darken and his shoulders move toward her. His breath froze as the knife in his hand moved immeasurably slowly and the world stopped around them. She held the shoe high and bore it down. The heel pierced the soft, pudgy flesh of the man's neck.

Blood pulsed from the hole she'd left as she drew the shoe back and slammed it down again.

The man fell as the red fountain sprayed from him, coating the clothes to her right. In a few beats, it slowed. The pool of crimson blood grew around him, staining the faux fur area rug that adorned the closet floor.

She stared at the shoe that was protruding from the man's neck. The swooping swan-style jewels on the shoe were covered in tiny drops of blood.

Dang.

She'd always loved those shoes, even though they were too narrow and had done nothing but sit in her closet since the day she'd bought them.

At least she had finally gotten her money's worth.

No matter what—or who—was to come, she couldn't be taken by surprise again.

Chapter Five

"Oh," Jarrod said, standing at the doorway of the closet. He held the towel tight around his waist as he stared at the scene in front of him. "Yeah. Okay," he said, stunned by what was unfolding.

"I… I…" Mindy stammered, pointing at the dead man on the floor.

"It's okay," he said, sidestepping around the man's body and moving to her. Like him, she was wearing nothing more than a white bath sheet. "Don't worry about this," he said, looking down at the knife that still rested in the fat man's hand. "Are you okay? He didn't cut you anywhere, did he?"

She seemed surprised, as though she hadn't even thought to check her body for any harm. She glanced down at her body, inspecting it. "I… I think I'm fine. Just… I don't know."

"You're in shock. This is normal. You have been through a lot in the last forty-eight hours."

He took her gently by the arm and helped her navigate around the body and out of the closet. "Let's just get you into the shower and then we'll get out of here."

There was blood on her hands and splattered over her white towel. In an effort to keep her from being even more traumatized, he moved her through the bathroom and kept her from seeing herself in the mirror. He let go of her and turned his back. "Hand me the towel. Then get in. I'll get you some clothes. Anything you prefer?"

His question was met with silence. After a moment, there was the click as she opened the shower door, and then she gently handed him the towel.

He walked out of the bathroom, loudly closing the door behind him so she could be more comfortable. He made his way back to her closet and the body.

The dead guy was in his midthirties, obese and starting to bald. His features were familiar, but he wasn't sure from exactly where.

There was no way anyone from the Gray Wolves could have known where he would be, or with whom, unless they had been following him. It didn't seem possible. This man had to be here for her.

Which brought him back to the reality that, regardless of any feelings he held for the woman, he couldn't do anything about them. He had to find out the truth and that was that.

He sent a quick email, with picture, to his people at the CIA and followed it up with an email to Zoey. Between his teams, it would only be a matter of time before he had an ID on this guy. Meanwhile, he had to get her out of this apartment and out of New York.

Only one safe place came to mind—Montana.

The Widow Maker Ranch, his family's new acquisition, was the safest place he could think of. There, they would be surrounded by family and out of the limelight.

However, if Mindy was more involved in the underbelly of the gun world than he assumed, it might well be like inviting the fox into the henhouse.

There were plenty of people on the lookout for him and his family. There had to be a bounty on their heads.

He couldn't bring trouble back to his family.

But where else could he take her? She was a somewhat well-known figure in the world, had been in her fair share of magazines as an up-and-coming heiress to the H&K fortune. He had even once seen her on the pages of *People* at a benefit at the Met. Anonymity would be hard to come by.

She was a major liability no matter where they went or what he chose to do with her.

His phone buzzed with an email from his handler at the CIA acknowledging what had gone down. Thankfully, they would take care of the body and get rid of any evidence once he and Mindy left.

At the far corner of her closet, there was a rack of men's suits and incidentals. He glanced down at his towel. He had planned on calling out for fresh clothes, but they didn't need anyone else coming or going from this house.

He grabbed a pair of the suit pants and a white button-up shirt. He'd have to go commando. Even if he found some skivvies around there, putting on another man's underwear was a step too far. The pants were a size too large and the shirt was a bit snug in the shoulders, but both would work well enough to get them out of this place and onto a flight—anywhere away from here.

He grabbed her a pair of jeans and a comfortable-looking shirt. The top had little blue flowers, bright and cheery but still tasteful—just like the woman it belonged to. Hopefully, he wasn't way off the mark and she'd like what he'd picked out. He glanced down to the clothes she had dropped on the floor. They were similar. Good. But what if they would remind her of what happened?

He grabbed a floral print dress as a second option for her. It was pretty, and he was sure that she would look beautiful in whatever outfit she chose.

And for the first time in his life, he chastised himself for not knowing more about women's fashion.

He set the clothes on her bed. The entire room was huge, and the bed at its heart reminded him of a sled skating on a gray wooden tundra. At the foot of her bed was a faux fur throw blanket, much like the one that lay under the corpse in her closet.

His fingers brushed against the blanket as he laid out her clothing. It was so soft, comforting… perfect for making love.

No. He couldn't go there.

He dropped his clothes onto the bed beside hers and started getting dressed. As he did up the last button, his mind wandered to who had worn these clothes before him. Their mere presence meant that she had allowed some guy to have his personal items here, and yet she hadn't mentioned any significant other. Neither had her file. According to what his handler had given him, her last major relationship had been five years ago to an investment banker who now worked on Wall Street. The guy had grown up with a silver spoon and went to NYU on a full ride, no doubt thanks to his family's donations to the dean of admissions' retirement fund.

On the other hand, it was possible that these clothes belonged to a new man, someone that the agency didn't know about. They certainly weren't infallible.

He shook his head. This woman and her world were a million miles apart from where he had come from and where he was going. She was an American princess and he only got close to her world by being a hired gun for the American government.

However, if push came to shove, his life seemed better; at least he was free to do whatever he wanted without falling under scrutiny from John Q. Public. Whatever she did, she probably had to answer to her board of directors, the tabloids, Twitter, Instagram, Facebook and, until recently, her brother.

He needed to tell her. Or, at the very least, she needed to find out.

She walked from the bathroom, toweling her hair dry. He hadn't thought a woman with wet hair was sexy before, but with her standing there, dabbing at her water-darkened locks, she looked like something out of a vintage magazine ad. With red lipstick, she could have been a spitting image.

When she saw him, she stopped in her tracks. "Oh." She stared, no doubt because of the clothes he was wearing. "I… I'm glad you found those. I had totally forgotten I even had them."

"I was hoping you or your boyfriend wouldn't mind." He silently prayed that she would put his nonsensical fears that she was seeing someone else to rest.

"Don't worry, there's no boyfriend."

"Do you have a lover…anyone that may come knocking at the wrong time?" He felt stupid for saying the word *lover*. Even to his own ears it sounded archaic and laced with Victorian-style prudence.

Her brow arched and she looked at him like she had heard something in his tone she didn't appreciate. A droplet of water slipped down from her forehead, dotting the edge of her hairline and sliding its way along her neck until it stopped at the perfect V-shaped hollow at the base of her throat.

Hell, he wanted to kiss that droplet away. He could imagine it now, moving closer to her. Pulling her into his arms. Licking away the drop from her skin. It probably tasted sweet thanks to her shower, maybe even smelled of some exotic flower. His body stirred to life at the thought.

He turned away, wishing that he'd had boxers on after all.

"No. No one like that," she said, walking behind him and moving to her sleigh-like bed. "Don't turn around, I'm going to get dressed."

There was the sound of her towel dropping to the floor behind him. Desire dictated that he turn, but respect stopped him from listening to his baser instincts…no matter how badly he wanted to scoop her into his arms and throw her onto the fur on the bed and make love.

He caught a glimpse of her, from her shoulders up, in the glass of a framed photo. If he moved just a bit he was sure that he could have a full view of her, but he forced himself not to. He didn't need any more reminders of how sexy she was and how badly he wanted her.

"I called a friend at the DOJ. If you want, I think we have somewhere we can go. Somewhere you will be safe," he said, forcing himself back to the task at hand.

"What about *him*?" she asked, motioning in the direction of the body.

"Don't worry. I told them what happened. For now, you aren't in any trouble, but they may want to question you. In the meantime, they just want you to get somewhere safe."

"And they put you in charge of that? Ever since I met you, people have been dropping like flies around me. I think I might be safer just getting away from you."

He snorted. He couldn't tell her the truth of who he was or why he was here—he'd be directly out on his ass if he did—but that didn't mean he couldn't hint. "Don't start looking over here to find the cause of what has been happening. I'm just a simple civil servant. Who would want to come after me?" he lied.

"When that man came at me, he said that I could 'thank my boyfriend' or something," she said, her voice muffled as he assumed she pulled her shirt on over her face. "I think he was talking about you."

"It's not likely. No one in the world would think we were in a relationship."

"Oh," she said, and there was a twinge of hurt in her voice. "I guess you're right, but who else could he have been talking about?" She walked close to him on her way to the bureau, where she grabbed a pair of light socks. She slipped them on—but before her feet disappeared, he made out the white tips of a fresh pedicure. This lady must have lived one hell of a life.

He shrugged. "Who knows what this guy was thinking. Until we get a positive ID on him, it's going to be hard to know anything. He didn't give you any other clues, did he?"

"Did you pat him down or whatever?"

"Yeah, there was nothing. Would've been nice if the bastard had carried a wallet, huh?" He chuckled.

"With whatever it is that you do, do you deal with this kind of thing a lot? I mean dead guys and stuff?"

He'd seen more death than he would ever care to admit. He'd spent more than one afternoon standing on-site at mass graves in the Fertile Crescent.

The most recent had been in Syria after a chemical weapons attack by the local government. He could still recall the stench of the bodies, the clouded, shrunken eyes of the dead and the hum of flies… oh, the flies. They alone could have been the stuff of nightmares.

"Are you okay?" she asked, touching his arm with her shower-warmed fingers.

"Yeah, fine. I guess I'm more tired than I thought I was. Hell of a week, this one." He located a suitcase in her closet and brought it out to her. "Pack what you are going to need."

"How long do you think we're going to be away? Wait… You're going to stay with me, aren't you, Chief Security Advisor?"

He smiled, and part of the protective coating on his heart chipped away. "You got it. At least, if that's what you want."

Her fingers moved down the hair of his arms, leaving a burning trail behind. "There is nothing that I would want more, though…" She paused.

"What?" he asked, touching his arm where her fingers had just been.

"I need to get in touch with my brother before I go anywhere." She opened her bag, completely unaware of the turmoil within him. "I tried to call him earlier, but it went to voice mail."

Now he wasn't so sure that he wanted to tell her about her brother's death after all. All of his normal interrogation techniques and practices were quickly plummeting out the window. He had to stop breaking the rules when it came to this woman. Though their circumstances were about as unconventional as they were uncomfortable, he had to try to get them back on track.

However, he had a feeling that she was already scared enough as it was, even without knowing that her brother had been gunned down by an agent.

He couldn't believe he had gotten himself so compromised with this woman, and so quickly. This wasn't his way. Normally, he was in, out and done. One day, one interrogation, one paycheck, and then shipped off to the next location. It was the way he liked it. Wham, bam, thank you, ma'am.

As it was, they had already spent more than their fair share of time together. He'd hate to think the effect she'd have on him in a week if he did decide to take her to Montana.

"Why don't you try to call him again?" he asked, feeling sheepish in feigning such deplorable ignorance.

She couldn't find out what he knew or his role in this. She would hate him forever if she did.

She walked over to the head of her bed, picked up the phone and dialed.

"I'm going to go make some phone calls of my

own. I'll come get you when I'm done," he said, walking out of her bedroom.

She nodded, but she was distant, no doubt worrying about her inability to get in touch with her brother.

He called his sister Zoey, but she didn't answer and his mind instantly moved to what Mindy must have been feeling. His gut ached. There was no way, absolutely no way he could be the one to break the news to her. Maybe she didn't need to know right now.

But if he didn't tell her, she might not agree to seek safety. They'd be back to square one.

And if she found out, she would be an even bigger wreck. He would have to console her. And as much as he desired to bring her into his arms, he had to stick to his guns and try to keep her in the professional zone.

He texted Zoey a message and instructions. Hopefully, she would come through. If not, they would probably be staying in New York—the heart of the target. If they did, he wasn't sure he could save her from being taken down if their enemy's aim was true.

Chapter Six

She stared at the receiver. Daniel's voice mail.
Again.

Something was definitely wrong. She hung up
and dialed his house. His live-in nanny, Esmerelda,
picked up. "Hey, Mindy, how's it going?"

"I'm okay," she lied, throwing things in her suitcase in a feeble attempt to pack. "Hey, you haven't
talked to Daniel today, have you?"

"Actually, he hasn't been home for a few days.
As far as I knew, he was supposed to be home last
night." There was the sound of a washing machine
in the background, reminding Mindy of all that
Daniel's life entailed—a life that was a far cry from
her own.

The flicker of panic she had been feeling grew
into a full-blown flame. "And you haven't heard
from him?"

"Nope, I tried calling him this morning. Anya

wanted to talk to him, but it went straight to voice mail."

Mindy glanced in the direction of her closet. What if he had been jumped, as well?

"I'll be there in a few. Please pack Anya a bag." She hung up the phone without waiting for Esmerelda to answer. She could apologize for her gruffness later; for now they had to get the hell out of there.

She walked downstairs with her suitcase and made her way into the living room, where Jarrod was waiting. His foot was tapping as he typed something on his phone. He was frowning as he worked.

Though he was incredibly handsome, he almost edged on a hot mess. Strangely enough, it was endearing, the way his hair matted against the side of his head and how his shirt was tucked in the back. She would've hated it if he had been perfect while she was so characteristically out of sync with her normal life.

"Jarrod?" she asked, her voice soft and unassuming. If she was going to have him help her with Anya, she needed to present this to him as gently as possible. If Jarrod was like most guys she'd known, having a child in tow would be the last thing he'd want.

He looked up from his phone. "Perfect." He hurried over to her, grabbing her suitcase and wheeling toward the door. "Let's go."

Making their way outside, they waved down a taxi. As Jarrod put her suitcase in the trunk, she gave the driver directions to her brother's house in New York. Jarrod sat down next to her in the back seat. Though there was enough room between them to fit another person, she suddenly felt entirely too close to him.

As they drove through the borough, Jarrod seemed glued to his phone.

"Is everything okay?" Mindy asked.

He clicked off his phone and looked over at her. "Yeah, it'll be fine. Just making sure we have airline tickets and everything is in order when we arrive at LaGuardia."

"Actually, we're going to need a third ticket." She gave him a guilty grin. "I want to take my niece with us, wherever it is we're going. I still haven't been able to reach Daniel, and I'm afraid something might've happened to him."

Jarrod's eyes widened slightly. "Your brother has a daughter?"

"If your friends at the DOJ don't let us take her, I don't think I can go. I need to make sure she stays safe. And if my family is under attack, it's vital she be protected."

"I see." He nodded as he chewed on the inside of his cheek. "How old is she?"

"She's five." Mindy paused, unsure of exactly how much she should tell him about her niece.

"Okay, I'll make sure she has a ticket with us."

Surprisingly, he didn't sound as upset as she had assumed he would be. Maybe he really wasn't interested in her as anything more than a job. In a way the realization came as a relief, even as disappointment also swirled through her.

"There's something else," she continued. "Anya has special needs."

"Allergies?"

"Actually, she has Down syndrome. We have to get her. I need to make sure she is safe."

He looked at her for a moment. "That's fine, but we're going to have to move some things around."

"I think it would be for the best."

"Do you think she's going to be worried about her father?" Jarrod asked.

"Well, I'm sure she's going to notice that her father is missing. He doesn't spend a lot of time with her, but he's really been trying ever since he..."

"He what?" Jarrod asked.

"Anya's mother wasn't from the United States." Mindy tensed. "At the time of Anya's birth, she was living in Russia. When Daniel heard he had a daughter, he tried to convince the woman to bring her to the United States, as the care and resources are better. Instead, the woman tried to extort money from him...to the tune of $1 million."

"Did he give it to her?"

She nodded. "He wouldn't refuse her money to take care of their daughter. However, it soon came to light that instead of using the money for their child, she put Anya up for adoption."

There was a long silence between them and the air was filled with the wailing of ambulances and the constant street noise of the city. She wished he would say something to give her an idea of what he was thinking.

"Does your family have this kind of drama?" She tried to laugh, but the sound came out strangled.

He snickered. "Every family brings their own kind of drama, but there is no family out there that doesn't have issues."

She would take that as a yes.

The taxi came to a stop in front of her brother's building. Jarrod seemed a bit surprised, but helped her out of the cab and grabbed her bag as she made her way toward the building.

The doorman welcomed her with a warm greeting, but she didn't hear exactly what he said so she just smiled. Jarrod followed behind her as they made their way over to the bank of elevators. She didn't have to say anything to the man waiting inside. He pushed the button for her brother's floor.

Again Jarrod seemed surprised, this time probably at the level of service, which once again made her wonder exactly how and where he had grown up. He'd said something about the Bronx, though he hadn't gone into a lot of detail. Maybe that was a good thing.

"Anya is a sweetheart. You are going to really like her," she said. "Do you know where we are going to go?"

Jarrod glanced at the bellhop and his features darkened, almost as though he was afraid the man was listening into their conversation—which, undoubtedly, he was.

"I'm so excited about a little vacation," she said, trying to cover her mistake. "I'm thinking Rio will be nice this time of year."

He looked bemused at her feeble attempt.

Thankfully, it didn't take long to get to the tenth floor. Esmerelda was waiting at the door when she knocked. "Hey," she said, opening the door. "Who's your friend?" She gave Jarrod an admiring glance.

"I'm just her driver, ma'am," Jarrod said. "But it is wonderful to meet you." He sounded prim and proper, matching the almost-fitting suit he was wearing.

Mindy tried to disguise her surprise.

"Well, it's nice to meet you, driver." Esmerelda gave him a nod.

"Is Anya ready to go?" Mindy asked.

"She should be. I put her in charge of picking a

few stuffed animals she would like to take along."
Esmerelda turned and walked toward Anya's bedroom. "How long are you planning on keeping
her?"

"I don't know, maybe a week. I'll try and get
ahold of Daniel again, but if you talk to him first…
just let him know she's with me." She was careful
not to reveal any unnecessary details.

Anya was sitting on the floor in her room.
She was coloring, her wide strokes spreading off
the edges of the paper and into the area rug, but,
thanks to the brand, they weren't leaving marks
behind.

"Anya, sweetheart," Mindy said, moving beside the girl and sitting down next to her. "How
are you doing, honey?"

Her brunette head popped up and she gave
Mindy a look of pure, unfiltered love. "Anta!" she
cried, using the name she had recently assigned
her. Anya smiled, her round face filled with joy as
she jumped up and looped her arms around Mindy's
neck. "Presents?"

Mindy laughed. Of course, that would be the
one word the five-year-old would say perfectly.

"Not today, sweetheart."

Anya let go and went back to her coloring.
Sometimes Mindy had to force herself to remember not to feel guilty or hurt. Anya was always
going to be a girl who wouldn't mask her true

feelings. And right now, that honesty was to be respected.

"Anya?" she said, trying to draw her attention, but Anya was concentrating on a horse on the paper. "Anya, I was hoping that you would want to go with me on an adventure. Are you all ready to go?" she asked, careful to make it something they both wanted. The last thing she needed was for the girl to have a meltdown. Time was not on their side.

Anya stood up and, without saying a word, ran to her bed. She grabbed a stuffed unicorn, complete with big sparkly eyes. "Let's go." She walked to Mindy and threw her hands up in the air, wanting to be picked up.

Hopefully, Daniel was fine. But in case they were right and Daniel was…*compromised*…this was the only option she had. And yet, it felt strange to put her trust in Jarrod, a man she had only just met. However, he was a man who had already risked his life for her. He had known what to do with the dead man in her closet.

Her brother would probably have something cynical to say when he found out about her relationship with Jarrod. He would certainly question the man's motives.

As much as she realized she ought to, she hated to let her mind slip to those thoughts. There were already enough questions roaring through her. Right now, she needed answers.

As she lifted the little one and hugged her to her chest, there was no question in her mind—when it came to this child, the only answer was to do anything to keep her niece safe, even if it meant placing her trust in a man she barely knew.

Chapter Seven

He had planned on the two of them simply boarding a plane and hightailing it out of there, masked by the anonymity of airport crowds. That was no longer an option. As soon as they walked out of Daniel's apartment pushing Anya in the stroller, all eyes were on them. It was like no one had ever seen a kid with special needs before and it irritated the hell out of him. He couldn't imagine what it must have been like for Mindy, having to deal with the sideways glances and hateful comments that she probably received when she was with Anya.

As they waited for their Uber, he glanced down the road, looking for anyone or anything that seemed out of the ordinary. Most were consumed by their phones, chatting away as they passed through their day glued to the screen. As much as he hated it, he was no different from anyone else in that regard. His job required he be accessible.

Anya babbled away in her stroller, laughing

sporadically at her private jokes. He had so many questions for Mindy about the little girl, but he didn't want to be anything like those people who treated Anya as some kind of curiosity instead of just a child. Whatever he needed to know, she would inevitably tell him or he would learn himself.

"Hi, baby girl, are you hungry?" He put his fingers to his mouth in a feeble attempt to sign.

Anya kicked her feet, sending one of her sandals into the gutter.

"Hey now," he said, running after the shoe. "You're going to need those if you're going on an adventure with us." He pointed up at the sky. "We're going to go on a plane. Have you ever been on a plane?"

The girl stared at him with her beautiful, round blue eyes and then glanced to Mindy, as though she were looking to her aunt for answers.

"You can talk to him, sweetie. Mr. Jarrod is a very nice man," she said, sending him a sweet smile.

"Mister? Wowzah, Anya, can you believe it? I'm a mister!" he said in mock surprise. "I gotta say, I've been called lots of things but never Mr. Jarrod. It has a pretty nice ring to it." He smiled at the little girl as he gently pushed a stray bit of hair out of her mouth where it had been trapped in a bit of syrup that must have been from this morning's breakfast.

"You nice?" Anya frowned.

"Most of the time. Yep, I'm pretty nice," he said, but as he spoke his thoughts moved to all of his days spent in war zones and pulling the trigger when the jobs had called for it.

He couldn't help but find it just a bit strange that to many, he was the man of their nightmares, and yet here he was getting an opportunity to play the hero. He could get used to this.

"Do you have puppy?" Anya asked, still very serious.

He smiled. "Um, nope. But someday, maybe. Do you like puppies?"

She gave him a vigorous nod. "I wanna puppy."

He glanced around, keeping an eye on their surroundings. There was a man standing at the corner who kept looking over at them. As Jarrod watched him, the man turned back to the phone in his hand.

Jarrod's phone pinged. It looked as though, thanks to the addition of his new ward, Zoey had gotten them a private plane. Not only would he get to hang out with a beautiful woman and her cute niece, it also looked like they would be flying in style. Things were starting to look up.

His phone pinged again. The driver had canceled.

Strike the looking-up thing. He ordered another

car, but they were ten minutes out. Hopefully, they wouldn't get close to arriving and cancel as the last driver had.

"I no go." Anya reached down and started to fumble with the buckle that was holding her small frame. "No, no, no." She repeated over and over.

"Anya, you can't get out of the stroller, sweetheart." Mindy squatted down on the other side. "You need to stay in there while we wait." She reached under the stroller and took out a bag of fruit snacks from her purse.

"I don't go," Anya said, smacking the crackers out of Mindy's hand and sending them flying across the concrete sidewalk.

A dark-haired woman in a long coat looked down at Anya and sneered. She slowed as she stepped over the mess on the sidewalk. "You know, they have genetic testing," she said, like they had committed some kind of crime by choosing to have Anya.

The comment pierced his heart in a way he had never experienced. "Who do you think you are, lady?"

"I'm someone who would never saddle a kid with a life like that."

The woman had no right to speak as she had— what did she know?

"Love doesn't count chromosomes. So why don't you just keep walking, you piece of trash,"

Mindy said, standing up and lunging toward the woman like she was about to pummel her.

The woman hurried away, likely returning to the bowels of hell where she had ascended from.

He was taken aback by Mindy's sudden shift into mama-bear mode. When she turned back to face him, her cheeks were red and there were tears dotting the corners of her eyes. She dabbed them away with the backs of her hands.

She came back to Anya, who was still fumbling with her belt. "Anya, baby," she cooed.

Anya looked up with a frown on her face. He wasn't sure if the girl understood what the woman had said, but he hoped that for her own sake she hadn't. Anya was already going to have a hard enough time without having to face the judgmental and negative attitudes of others who had no business talking.

"I no go," she said, seemingly oblivious to the melee that had occurred.

"Where don't you want to go?" he asked, trying to give Mindy a moment to collect her rage and blink back her tears, though she had every right to be angry.

Anya threw her hands down to her sides and huffed, looking up at the sky like the mere question was exasperating. "No. Planes. No."

"Are you afraid of flying?" he asked.

She wiggled back and forth in her seat as though she could get out that way. "I go kinder."

He gave Mindy a confused look.

She sighed. "Honey, we can't go to Kinder-musik today."

"I wanna bell. Bell!" Anya screamed at the top of her lungs.

In case they weren't already being gawked at, now they had everyone's attention.

"Anya, we don't get to play music today. No." Mindy shook her head, unflappable against the five-year-old's will.

"Anta, I wanna play," Anya repeated, giving her a pleading look.

He would have found it impossible to say no to that face, but Mindy just shook her head.

Anya started to cry, loud and long wails.

"You know, we have a private plane. I'm sure that we can wait an hour or two before we have to take off," he said, watching in agony as Anya's temper tantrum spiraled out of control.

Mindy tried to comfort her. She whispered softly in the girl's ear, but instead of calming her, it seemed to have the opposite effect.

Mindy glanced up at him. "You really don't mind?"

"Absolutely not." He glanced down at his phone. An hour one way or the other wouldn't pose a problem. Time wasn't their enemy; rather, it was the unknown. Maybe while they were taking a break he could check into things, talk to his sister and his contacts, and see if he could get a little further in their investigation.

On the other hand, he wasn't sure giving in to the girl's temper tantrum was the right strategy. If they gave in now she would use the same strategy to wear them down anytime she didn't get her way. But, for right now it seemed like going to the music thing was the only option that would calm her down.

"Is it within walking distance?" he asked.

"Yeah, it's only a couple of blocks. If we hurry, we can still make it on time." She checked her watch. "Anya doesn't do well with spontaneity." She gave him a pinched look.

He canceled the Uber. "It's okay, I know plenty of people who take change even worse than her." On occasion, that someone was him.

A class where children played kazoos and snare drums sounded like an instant headache, but he wasn't about to let Anya down. She was already going to go through so much change in her life, thanks to the death of her father....

His chest ached as he realized how big a role he had inadvertently played in altering this girl's life forever. He owed her a debt far greater than he could ever repay. Sitting through a developmental class seemed inconsequential in comparison.

As they walked to the class, passersby continued to stare at their impromptu family.

"Is this normal?" he asked, motioning in the direction of an older woman who was craning her neck in order to look into their stroller.

"I know what you mean," Mindy said, glancing around them at the people who were suddenly no longer staring. "I'm still getting used to it, too. Anya has only been living with Daniel for about six months, and I only get to see her a few days a week." She paused for a moment. "I hope I didn't embarrass you back there...you know, with the woman and all. I should have had better control over my emotions. But, seriously, that woman deserved a smack to the jaw."

"I don't disagree with you in the slightest. Actually, I thought it was sexy as hell." He gave her a wide, alluring smile.

She cocked her head, looking at him like she wasn't sure whether or not he was teasing.

He raised his hand in testament to his truth. "No, really."

She laughed and, reaching over, she took his hand and lowered it. "Only you." Instead of letting go, she slipped her fingers between his and let their interlaced hands move between them. "It takes a special kind of man to watch his *friend* nearly take a woman down, and then like her more for it."

"First, she was abhorrent; and second, I'm

nothing if not special…in everything I do," he said, chuckling.

"Oh, you are a cocky one, aren't you?" She giggled, the sound high and full of perfect happiness, and a little more of his hard shell chipped away.

Walking hand in hand with her at his side while they pushed the stroller, it struck him how much they appeared to be a family. The thought thrilled him just as much as it terrified him. In a way, it reminded him of everyone waiting for him back in Montana.

He could still remember the day his parents had brought the twins, Trish and Chad, home. They had been such little things that in his six-year-old mind he had thought they were dolls…that was, until Trish had started crying. A lump rose in his throat.

His phone pinged. Zoey. Of course, she would text him the moment he had even a tiny thought about his other sister.

Zoey was checking their status. Letting go of Mindy's hand, he texted her back, telling her about what had come up. As it was, it would be a quick flight into Missoula compared to commercial flights, which would not have landed until close to midnight.

He slipped his phone back in his pocket.

"Everything okay?" Mindy motioned to his phone. "Your girlfriend looking for you?"

He lost his footing, tripping himself, then quickly correcting with a nervous laugh. "Uh, ha. No. It was my sister."

"Sure."

"What, are you jealous or something?"

"Ha." She maneuvered the stroller over the curb as they crossed the street. "Are you always this full of yourself, or are you being this way just for my benefit?"

He wasn't sure of the right answer. "If you play your cards right, everything I do could be for your benefit."

She stopped and stared at him, a shocked grin on her face. "Wow. Just…wow." She gave an amused sigh.

He was just as surprised as she was that he had said it. He didn't have room in his life for a full-blown family. Right now he didn't even have a lifestyle that would work for a pet.

"You know you don't mean that," she said, starting to walk again.

Though she was right to call him out, he wasn't sure she wasn't wrong. He had a habit of saying exactly what he meant, in fact to the point that sometimes people called him callous for his lack of filter between his brain and his mouth. Then, he'd always thought it best to let people know where they stood with him—at least when it came to his private life.

Again, he reminded himself that this woman and this child were work.

Yes, she was right. He hadn't meant it. He *couldn't* mean it, no matter how badly a part of him yearned to have a typical America life.

He was grateful as they rounded the corner and saw a brightly colored sign for Kindermusik. He walked ahead and opened the door for them.

"You ready for this fun?" Mindy asked with a wink.

Thanks to their arrival into his life, as far as he was concerned, the fun had already started.

Chapter Eight

Though Mindy had taken Anya to her music class twice before, she didn't remember it being quite so loud. A little boy was sitting over in the corner, waiting with his mother for class to start, slapping two pieces of wood together and screaming at the top of his lungs. Not far from him was a girl with tears streaming down her face, her whining approaching the decibels that only dogs and bats could hear.

A group of toddlers ran around her legs, brushing against them as she unstrapped a wiggling Anya from her stroller. As soon as her feet touched the ground, Anya toddled after the kids in vain hopes of catching up.

"Hey," she called after them, but none of the children paid her any mind. "Anya here. Hey!" she yelled, but as she hurried she tripped and fell to her knees. She crawled for a few feet then, giving up, sat and watched the kids make another lap around the waiting room.

The boy in the corner stopped screaming just long enough to look at her, then picked up his wailing again.

"Oh. Wow. No." Jarrod backed up until he was pressed against the wall. Terror marked his features.

"Yes, this is happening. Remember, you agreed that we should be here," she said, raising one eyebrow.

"Yeah, I clearly lost my freaking mind." He motioned toward a child who was actively doing something in their diaper. "I am not emotionally prepared for this. No."

The distinct aroma of a full diaper wafted over. She tried to ignore it, but she could have sworn that it was growing more pungent by the second. Just as she was about to concede that, like Jarrod, this was the last place she wanted to be, the door to the back opened. A woman in her midfifties with bottle-red hair and a yellow broom skirt stepped out. Her neck was adorned with a variety of macaroni necklaces that were likely made by the throngs of children who passed through her doors every day.

"Children, children," she said in a quiet, singsong voice. "One, two, three, eyes on me."

The kids quieted down and stopped running.

The woman clapped, the sound as gentle and

reminiscent of Mr. Rogers as her voice. "Well done, my little butterflies."

Mindy could feel Jarrod rolling his eyes next to her. She couldn't blame him. For a man like him, who was clearly more comfortable kicking ass and taking names, standing through this musical, artistic lovefest probably felt just about as comfortable as a colonoscopy.

She giggled.

The front door to the shop jingled and a man wearing a red shirt walked in. The little girl in his arms was crying and her face was contorted with rage as she attempted to wiggle free from his grasp. From the look of things the girl was in the throes of a nuclear meltdown.

The instructor glanced over at them, and as the little girl saw the woman, she quieted down.

"My name is Lily Lilac Peppercorn," the baby-whispering instructor said.

Oh, that name had to be so fake.

"I'm your instructor today with my little helper…" She pulled her other hand out from behind her back and a sock puppet with blue hair came into view. Together the woman and the puppet made all the colors of the rainbow. Just when Mindy thought things couldn't get worse.

"This is Jacques. Jacques, can you say hi?" The woman wiggled her thumb and the puppet jerked violently.

A few of the kids cheered at the unexpected assistant, but one or two moved into their nanny's legs. At least, she assumed the women at their sides were their nannies. She glanced around. Jarrod was one of only two men. The rest of the caregivers were women, and most had the look of paid help. A couple were even complete with candy striper–like uniforms. It made sense. Few of the people in her social circles who had kids were ever seen with them. They had staff to take care of their children's daily needs and requirements.

Ms. Peppercorn kept talking in her singsong voice as Mindy walked over to Anya and scooped her up into her arms. Though she was five, she was markedly smaller than the rest of those in her age group. Anya clapped her hands on each side of Mindy's face, joyfully playing a beat to the tune of the woman's voice.

Maybe it wouldn't be so bad after all.

"Why don't you all follow me in so we can get started," the woman said, giving the kids little waves as they flooded through the doors with their caregivers.

Mindy walked forward but stopped as she noticed that Jarrod wasn't behind her. She turned back. "Oh, come on now, there's no chance that I'm going to leave you out here while I go in." She took his hand and pulled him forward.

"I…but…" he protested.

"Emotionally ready or not, here we go," she said, smiling at him as Anya continued to play drums on her cheeks.

There was no way she could do this alone. As they walked into the room, the man in a red shirt elbowed his way through the crowd, almost as though he was trying to get closer to the only other man in the group.

Her mind turned to Daniel. He was normally the one to bring Anya down here, when he wasn't traveling for work. It was the one thing they normally did together, but since they had picked up the girl, Anya had yet to mention her father.

Part of Anya's personality was that she often wasn't as emotionally present as other children her age. It was just another of the facets of Anya's being that had proved to be more of a struggle than either she or Daniel had been prepared for.

When Mindy had learned about Anya's diagnosis, she had thought that it wouldn't be that hard to adapt their lives to meet her needs. If anything, she was bringing *extra* to their lives. Yes, she would need extra time, extra attention, extra love, but in return she would give them all the extras that they needed in their lives, as well. And though it had been harder than she had first anticipated, all the extras were worth it.

And yet, wasn't that what all relationships were based upon—the little extras? She gave

Anya a squeeze as she thought about how much she loved her.

She looked to Jarrod and thought about the things he had done for her just in the short time since they had met. As she watched him, he reached up and scratched at his scruffy goatee. He played with it, almost as though he were using the hair on his face to comfort himself in the same way a child would turn to a beloved teddy bear.

She didn't have time for a relationship. In many ways, having her niece in her life was significantly easier and far less dangerous for her heart than having a man. Though they both had the power to break her heart, Jarrod seemed far more likely to do so.

She glanced down at their hands and then up to his face. There were the start of fine lines around his eyes—he had the face of a man who had seen what life could bring. He was clearly a good man, but that didn't mean he saw the world the way she did, or that he could promise he would keep her heart safe if she chose to give it to him for safe-keeping.

But she was jumping ahead again. He had made no promises. He had barely hinted at anything beyond friendship. In fact, she barely knew this man. Still, even though they had just met, it didn't change the pull she felt every time she thought of him. She had to fight her feelings and pull them back before she was too far gone. Vulnerability wasn't a luxury she could afford. Not now. Not ever.

The lady leading the class handed out tambourines. Jarrod's face was pinched as he looked at the instrument. If she hadn't known better, she would have thought that someone had just handed him an active warhead—though, perhaps he would have looked slightly more at ease.

She sat Anya down and took her tambourine. "It's going to be okay, Jarrod. It's only an hour." She could have sworn he looked even more tormented at the mention of time.

"All right, everyone, let's sing while we count with our tambourines," the instructor said.

Surprisingly, Jarrod found the beat and pretty soon he was even helping Anya shake her tambourine in unison with the other children. After about ten minutes, and three songs and something Ms. Peppercorn called a happy heart yoga pose, Mindy saw the start of a smile on his face. Sure, he could act all tough and manly, but no man could resist the joy of seeing children completely enjoying themselves. She would have gone so far as to say he even looked comfortable.

And dang it if it didn't make her like him even more. By the end of the class, he was singing with Anya at the top of his lungs, and thankfully the tambourines had been put away. They'd gone through kazoos, drumsticks, whistles and harmonicas, and her head was throbbing. It didn't escape her that after all her teasing, she was the one paying the price for the cacophony. Karma was rearing its ugly head.

The man in the red shirt had moved closer during each song. And, out of the corner of her eye, she could see him watching Anya. In an attempt to shield her from the man's gaze, Mindy pulled Anya in closer to her legs and farther out of the man's field of vision.

As the class came to an end, the man kept looking over at them. The child beside him was peering up at him, and though they had seemed to enjoy themselves, the child looked almost frightened at the prospect of leaving with him. It struck her as odd, but she questioned herself for judging anyone with their child. She wasn't really a parent. She didn't know enough about kids to really understand exactly what dynamic was happening, so to jump to any conclusions was out of the question.

She nudged Jarrod. "Look at that guy," she said, motioning with her chin toward the man and the child.

As he glanced over at them, the little girl at the man's side rushed away from him and over to the instructor. The man frowned and looked over at them. He noticed them staring, and instead of going after the little girl and bringing her back, he moved toward the door. As he turned, Mindy made out the telltale bulge at the man's hip. He was carrying a gun.

The guy looked back at them, giving her a menacing grin and mouthed the words *you're dead.*

As they approached the man, one of the moms stepped in her way, saying something she barely heard about organic produce. She tried to push past her to go after the man, but the woman seemed hell-bent on telling her something about the health benefits of going vegan.

The man's hand dropped to his gun, like any minute he would start shooting.

The woman said something about asparagus.

Mindy bit her tongue, but all she wanted to do was tell the woman that no one cared, especially when there was a killer in their midst.

The man smirked and sidestepped out the door, their eyes locked until the moment he disappeared outside.

What in the hell was going on?

The little girl wrapped her arms around the instructor's legs as the rest of the children and their guardians streamed out of the room.

Jarrod moved after the man, but Mindy stopped him. "Wait…"

He looked as though he was about to argue but stopped and took a breath. "We need to get our hands on that man. Find out who he's with."

He was right, but as much as she wanted the

information, they had to get out of there. "For all we know, we are going to get jumped the second we walk out of here. We need to go somewhere we can be safe."

He chewed on the inside of his cheek. "If he's waiting outside, he's stupid."

"Anya," she said, leaning down, "are you ready to go?"

Anya stood up and wrapped her arms around her legs, just like she must have seen the other little girl do to the instructor.

"Do you know this little girl?" the instructor asked as she made her way over to them.

Mindy shook her head.

"She said she didn't know that man." The woman picked up the little girl and pulled her into her arms. The girl buried her blond head into the woman's neck, and her back shuddered as she sobbed. "He took her from the park. I bet it was the one two blocks down."

"Her mother…" Mindy said, looking to Jarrod as she thought of how the poor mother must be feeling right now, realizing that her daughter was gone. "If he's willing to kidnap a child without fear of reprisal, who knows what else he is capable of. He has to be found."

"Call the police," Jarrod said. "I'll see if I can get my hands on him before it's too late."

The instructor hurried to the phone and dialed

as he rushed out with Mindy and Anya behind him, leaving their stroller.

"Stay here," he said as they reached the sidewalk in front of the building. People brushed by, moving between them in their rush to get wherever they were going.

She shook her head. "You can't leave us."

"I'll be right back," he urged. "Really, my going alone is the only chance we have to catch this guy. Go back inside."

Though she wanted to keep her protector with her, she had to let him go. They had to find out what was really going on…and who their enemies were.

"Go." She waved him on. "But be safe."

Something about the way she looked at him, like she was torn between needing him and pushing him away, pulled at his heart. Her green eyes reflected the world around them, the masses of people and the confusion, but at their center was a call to him. If she asked for just about anything, he wasn't sure he could refuse her.

He was just lucky she wasn't asking for his heart.

Forcing himself to turn away, he rushed in the direction the man had gone.

The odds weren't in his favor, but he had to try. He wasn't the kind of man who could watch an innocent child be victimized and then do nothing about it. This man was a lowlife who seemed to believe it was acceptable to use a child as a weapon of war, and as far as he could tell, a war was exactly where they had found themselves.

And war was far better than being home. In war, he could cut down his enemy and watch as their blood peppered the ground. There was some amount of justice, unlike with Trish's death. Bayural prided himself at being untouchable. Which meant as soon as Jarrod went home to Montana, he would be forced to come face-to-face with his failure—and he wasn't a man who could fail.

About a block down he spotted the kidnapper. He thought about calling out, yelling for someone to grab the man, but most people weren't like him. Most didn't want to get their hands dirty. Most people put self-preservation above a call to arms given by an absolute stranger. Maybe people were smarter than him in that regard, but he knew how to grab life by the horns and ride it for all it had.

He didn't wait for the walk sign; instead, he ran, weaving through the slow-moving bumper-to-bumper traffic. The driver of a black Tundra honked as he dodged out in front of it. He smacked the hood as the vehicle sped up, forcing him to jump and slide over their hood. As his feet touched the ground, he flipped the driver the bird. The driver returned the motion with both hands.

Okay, so maybe Jarrod wasn't so different from other people. Just like the rest of the world, he wasn't above biting back. And, if he got his hands on the bastard who had kidnapped the girl, he would tear that sucker up.

The man in the red shirt turned and glanced in his direction at the sound of one last honk. Even from almost a block away, Jarrod could see the look of recognition on the man's face, but it quickly turned to a look of desperation.

Jarrod ran toward him, pushing his way through the crowd. It was at times like this that he wished he was back with his team. A quick call on the handset and this guy would have already been taken down to his knees. As it was, here he was playing a game of cat and mouse.

He lost sight of the man as he rushed in the direction he had last seen him. By the time he made it to the spot he'd seen the guy, he was gone.

Luckily, a woman in a frumpy brown wool peacoat pointed to the left. "He went that way. Into the deli."

He wasn't sure if he should listen to the woman. In a place like NYC it was sometimes hard to tell which side of the law a person cheered for. But her tip-off was all he had until the police showed up. That was if they showed up.

The girl hadn't been hurt, only abducted and a bit shaken up. In some circles, something like that barely warranted their becoming involved. There were murders waiting to be solved and kids that were actively missing. For them, this girl's story actually ended pretty well. But he didn't hold himself to the same standard. As jaded as he was by war and the travesties that came with it, he couldn't be just a passive observer.

He rushed into the deli. The place smelled like smoked meat and expensive cheese, and it was so packed with people that there was standing room only and even that was in high demand. The man must have known NYC to have picked such a popular deli, a deli where he could quickly disappear in the crowd and slip out of Jarrod's grasp. That was, assuming the guy was even in the place.

From where Jarrod stood, he could almost see the front counter through the rustling field of heads and shoulders. He wasn't a small man, but standing there in such close quarters with everyone else made him feel utterly insignificant.

This was hopeless. He should have just stayed out of this and ignored his need to be a hero. Perhaps his ego had run away with him in thinking he could make a difference. Here, without his family and team, he was only a single man standing against evil.

Or maybe he didn't have to be quite as alone. He pulled out his phone. He maneuvered between people until he spotted the guy in the red shirt near the back door, leading to the kitchen. He was scanning the crowd, no doubt searching for Jarrod.

Before the man had a chance to spot him, he snapped a picture. The kidnapper pressed open the swinging door and slipped into the back.

Beside Jarrod stood a man who had to be at least six foot seven and pushing three hundred pounds. Jarrod tried to go around him, but he moved to block Jarrod's path.

"Out of the way. Police business," Jarrod said, but as he moved to take a step the big man didn't budge.

Instead, he glowered down on him, anger and impatience in his eyes. "Sure," he said with a smirk. "Look, man, you can get in line like everyone else." He jerked his thumb in the direction of a nearly nonexistent line that was more a mash-up of bodies.

The man behind him nodded in agreement, and though he wasn't as big, he looked like he was itching for a fight.

"I'm not here for a damned sandwich. I'm here to do my job. Now get out of my way," he urged.

"Flash the badge or you get your ass to the back of the line, man," the tall guy said, and this time his voice took on a harder edge and his body stiffened as though he was preparing to throw a punch.

Though Jarrod was tough, looking at the guy's biceps made him question his prowess. The dude's arms were as thick as his thighs. One well-placed punch and he would be eating through a straw for at least a month.

Fighting this guy would be about as worthless as continuing the chase.

He had the kidnapper's picture. With Jarrod's team, that was just about as good as a death warrant.

Chapter Nine

She wasn't a doormat, no way. But right now, standing with Anya and staring down the sidewalk in the direction that Jarrod had disappeared, she felt weak.

It wasn't that she needed him, she reminded herself. No. What she *needed* was to know they were safe. And as much as she had thought she could protect herself, this week had proved otherwise.

And perhaps that was what made her feel weakest of all—she had been unable to save herself.

For her entire life, she had convinced herself that she could handle anything and that she was braver than most, and yet when the nerve agent had been thrown at them, she had merely stood there. Jarrod had saved her life.

And now, here he was seeking justice for a child he didn't even know, and soon he would be whisking them away to some unknown place where they would be out of the killer's sights.

If she could have willed his return, she would have. Anya fussed. "Hungry, Anta. Hungry."

"Okay, sweetie. We will get food soon."

"No. No. Now." She whined, the sound a screechy wail.

Mindy reached into her purse, fishing around for some kind of snack. At the bottom of her tote was a semi-crushed bag of Goldfish crackers Daniel had given her the last time she had watched Anya.

Anya, having seen the oily bag, opened and closed her starfish-like hands as her whine turned into desperate grunts.

"Don't eat all of them in one sitting," she said, handing Anya the bag. "When Jarrod gets back we will go get some food. Okay?"

Anya ignored her, instead she yanked the ziplock bag open, tearing the sides in her rush to get to the few whole Goldfish crackers that remained.

When Jarrod appeared in the distance she could have sworn the clouds broke and a sunbeam illuminated his presence.

He didn't look at her as he walked toward them, surrounded by strangers.

It always struck her how, in this city of millions, a person could still be all alone. In many ways, the way he looked, completely oblivious to the world around him, was how she often found herself feeling.

Sure, she had shirttail friends, and friends spread around the globe, but more often than not, she spent her time dealing with emails, invoices, patents and lawyers. And even when she did get the chance to hang with her friends, it was like they had all reached the same place in their careers…the point of no return.

Looking at Jarrod's muscular, sinewy arms and perfect V-shaped body, she couldn't help wondering if she had reached the same place with him, as well. There was no question about her level of attraction to him. It had been months, if not years, since she had felt this kind of burning inside of her when she looked at a man. And perhaps the best part was how much he appreciated that she was a smart, capable and professional woman.

Which reminded her… She tried to straighten her body and appear not to be in full-blown panic mode. He couldn't know all that she was feeling. If he did, he'd realize how unstable she felt.

As he approached she looked for signs that he'd been in a fight, but he appeared unscathed. A wave of relief washed through her, making her realize that it wasn't just her and Anya's safety she had been concerned with.

"Did he get arrested? Do we need to go to the station and give a statement or anything?" she asked in a single breath.

"What?" He looked at her like he was trying to decipher what exactly she had just blurted out.

"Did you get him?" She tried again, this time more measured.

His face contorted with anger and disappointment. "He got away, but I got a picture of him."

What would a picture do? It seemed utterly worthless. She thought of the old adage "a picture is worth a thousand words." Right now she could think of at least that many to tell him how disappointed she was that he let the kidnapper slip through his fingers.

Maybe he wasn't who she needed in a bodyguard after all.

"What happened?" She tried to not sound as if she was interrogating him, even though that was exactly what she was doing—or maybe, it was more of an interview for the job he was already doing for her.

"Whoever this guy is, he knows the city. He definitely used it to his advantage." Jarrod directed his attention down at Anya. "But don't worry, my team will track him down. My sister has already sent my brothers after him. By the end of the day I'm sure we'll know everything from this guy's cell phone number to the size of his shoes."

Though Jarrod seemed self-assured, she didn't want to point out that they were still trying to figure out exactly who had attacked them. If his siblings were as talented as he was making them out to be, it didn't seem right that they were still at a loss. Or maybe she was just being cynical.

"How's my girl Anya doing?" Jarrod asked, squatting down beside the girl, who was still digging into the bag.

Anya didn't bother to look up at him. Instead, she shoved a handful of crackers into her mouth.

"Are you hungry, sweetheart?" Jarrod asked.

Anya finally looked up at him and nodded. "Happy Meal?"

"No way," Mindy said.

As they made their way down the city block, it almost felt surreal. Only moments before, they had been chasing down a kidnapper. Now they were going on with their day as though nothing had happened. She couldn't make sense of her life. It seemed to ebb and flow between danger and safety in a way that made her almost question her sanity. She couldn't keep going on like this.

"Happy. Meal," Anya insisted.

Jarrod passed her a pleading look. He might not want to argue with the little one, but that didn't mean they could give in to Anya's whims. Things had a way of spiraling with her. If they didn't stand their ground now, Anya would learn that they were a soft touch. And the next time, when they really meant no, Anya would push even harder.

On the other hand, soon Anya would be back

with Daniel and her nanny and Mindy wouldn't have to deal with the repercussions. It might be a little passive-aggressive, but with the disappearing act Daniel was pulling, he kind of deserved it.

"I'm sorry, sweetheart," Mindy said. "But we'll get you something that will make your tummy happy."

Anya threw her arms over her chest in an angry huff.

For Anya, the reaction was mild. Finally Mindy was getting this caregiver thing down. The last time she had told Anya no, and actually stuck with it, the little one had gone into a full ten-on-the-Richter-scale tantrum, and Daniel had been forced to step in to handle things.

Hopefully, everything with Daniel was okay. It wasn't entirely unlike him to up and disappear for no reason, although since Anya arrived, he had been much more grounded. The last time he had done this was when he found out about Anya being put up for adoption. He had raced off to Russia without telling anyone and had returned with the girl under his wing.

Maybe he had another child out there, or he was rescuing someone she knew nothing about. For now, she would have to give him the benefit of the doubt and assume that his reckless behavior was nothing more than one of his flights of fancy. And yet there was a twinge of something inside of her that said there was more to this, that he was in danger.

She pushed the thought aside. Daniel was fine. She was making something out of nothing.

An Uber pulled up next to them, and the driver rolled down his window. "Are you Jarrod?"

Jarrod nodded. "Thanks for finding us."

The driver stopped just long enough for them to scurry into their seats before taking off to the airport. Anya sat in Mindy's lap, which was not ideal. If they needed to do any driving in their next location, she would need to find a car seat.

After making the Uber driver stop at a corner fruit stand and buying a bag of fruit for Anya, they made their way to the airport. They drove onto the tarmac where their private jet waited. As they got out, she made sure to hand the driver a hundred-dollar bill for adding the stop. The guy looked surprised at the money, but it disappeared into his pocket without protest.

She would have given almost anything to have an existence like their driver's. Sure, his life probably had its ups and downs, but instead of worrying about life and death, he had to worry about which bridge to avoid and where traffic was the lightest.

More than anything she wished she could just *be*.

The pilot welcomed them with a handshake and a smile before helping them board. He and Jarrod spoke to each other, but instead of speaking in English, it sounded something like French.

If only she had taken it in school. As it was, she felt like an outsider standing in the middle of their conversation.

The plane was larger than it looked, with two rows of leather airline seating in the front and couches in the back. In the farthest reaches of the plane there was a door, and even from where she stood she could see a bed adorned with a fresh-cut bouquet of sunflowers. Their giant droopy heads were perched on the pillow, sunny and warm in their welcome.

A flight attendant walked out of the back bedroom and nodded at Mindy and Anya. "Welcome, ma'am. If there is anything I can help you with, please do not hesitate to ask. Would you like a glass of champagne to get your flight started? Perhaps orange juice for Ms. Anya?"

"That would be wonderful, thank you," Mindy said. "Would you like one as well, Jarrod?"

He nodded, but his attention turned to Anya, who was pulling at his suit pants.

The attendant walked toward them and took the bag of fruit from her. "Would you like me to chop these up for you?"

She felt silly for having made them stop to get something for Anya. Of course there would be food on the private jet. Yet, from the way that Jarrod had talked about their flight, it had sounded more like a puddle jumper than something Hans Anders would have used to fly around the world.

It wasn't that she wasn't used to traveling in lavish style; it was just that Jarrod, with his rugged looks and penchant for danger, seemed like the opposite of posh. He seemed like the kind of guy who would be more comfortable holding one of her guns deep in the jungle somewhere, waiting and watching for the moment he could take someone out. At the same time, though, it was hotter than hell to see a badass like him surrounded by luxury. It was like she was getting the best of both worlds.

The flight attendant made her way to a small kitchenette near one of the couches in the back of the plane and started putting together their drinks, complete with gold-trimmed stemware.

"Go. Go," Anya said as she plopped down in the front seat.

"Do you want me to sit with you?" Mindy called to Anya.

Anya shook her head and pulled her stuffed unicorn from her backpack and buckled him in the seat next to her.

Mindy followed Jarrod down the narrow aisle, stopping when she came to Anya. She quickly buckled her seat belt. "You have to stay in your seat when we are flying. Unless you need to go potty. Okay?"

Anya didn't pay her any mind, instead pulling at her confining belt.

Mindy readjusted her purse as she stood up. Nestled inside was a diaper for the girl. Maybe she should have checked to see if she needed to be changed before they had gotten here. As it was, she only had a single diaper and it would hardly be enough for even a day, let alone however long it was going to be that they would be away. "Do you need to go potty now?"

Anya shook her head. "We go?" she said, her words somewhere between a question and a statement as she pointed out the window and toward the airplane's wings. "Dada?" she added.

Jarrod twitched, the action so minuscule that if Mindy hadn't been standing right behind him, she might have missed it.

"I…uh… We are hoping to meet up with your daddy soon." She tripped on the fear the words created within her. What if her feeling had been right and there really was something going on with her brother? What if he was hurt, or worse?

She looked over at Anya as she took the seat next to Jarrod. Anya was pulling at her wayward curls, wrapping her hair around her finger and letting go like her hair was just another of her toys. Anya looked over at her and smiled, the action so unexpected and pure that she felt her heart skip a beat. This was love.

And true of love, terror rested on its heels.

What if Daniel remained missing? Mindy wasn't sure she was ready or right for the job of being Anya's mom or guardian or caregiver. Sure, she knew how to help her, to guide her through the day, but being a mom was totally outside of her comfort zone. It was such a foreign concept that she couldn't even really imagine it.

Her thoughts moved to her own mother. It was strange, but she couldn't really remember exactly what she looked like, though she could still remember the scent of her mom's skin and her Shalimar perfume. She had always loved floral pantsuits and high heels, and no matter what was happening, she was always dressed to impress.

Her mother had completely bought into the myth that was "the perfect life." Go to school, work on herself, exercise, uphold societal beauty standards, marry, have children, get the dog and the white picket fence and then die. Well, all except she had raced to the finish line and had died when Mindy was merely eight years old.

She had been the one to find her mother in the bathtub, pills scattered around the marble floor. Even now, sometimes when she closed her eyes for the night, she could still see her mother's lifeless expression and her slack jaw…as if she had spoken her name one last time as she had slipped from this world and into the next.

Mindy couldn't imagine what her mother must have been going through to make such a choice, but she didn't hate her for it. If anything, she felt only a deep sadness and guilt. If only she had acted better, behaved better, listened better or paid more attention to her mother's instructions, perhaps her mother wouldn't have made the same choice. Now she understood those feelings were those of a child who thought that everything was her fault. But even with that acknowledgment and understanding, at her core she still felt guilty.

If she had been *more* for her mother, there was no way her mother could have left her.

She and Daniel had never really talked about her mother. Daniel's mother, her father's first wife, had attended the funeral, but instead of mourning she had mostly doted on her son. It had made Mindy dislike the woman in the moment, but over the coming years they had made progress with their relationship. Right up until she had shacked up with her pool boy, a man half her age, and turned away from Daniel.

There was nothing wrong with a woman choosing a younger man, but it was wrong that the woman had forgotten the son she had previously used as a crutch when he no longer served her purposes.

Which brought Mindy back to the impossibility of being a mother. She was totally not ready;

nor did it feel like she ever would be. Her life was a thing of beauty as it was. Everything, until recently, had been centered on logic. One decision led to another, which led to another. Each time she simply had to ask herself if the outcome fit their business model and marketing plans. If not, she made a different choice. Mothering was nothing but a series of ambiguities. And ambiguities were not something she was prepared to handle.

Not only that, but just looking at her and Daniel's mothers, maybe it was best if she didn't go down that road... If her life was anything like theirs, she could only see it ending in disaster.

The attendant brought them each a glass of champagne and Anya's orange juice, along with a peanut-butter-and-jelly sandwich—Anya's favorite. After Anya ate and went potty, Mindy had another glass of champagne and fell into the comfortable flight's lull.

Jarrod was doing something on his phone, and after about an hour Anya fell asleep, her head propped up against the window as if she were hoping that she could spend her dreams in the clouds. Mindy nudged Jarrod and smiled as she pointed across the aisle toward the girl.

"Ah, what a sweetheart. I bet we wore her out," he said.

"Why don't we move back to the couches, that

way we don't disturb her?" she whispered, un-buckling her seat belt.

Jarrod nodded and followed her. She couldn't help staring at the door that led to the bedroom. It was silly and completely asinine, but all she could imagine was slipping her hand in his and leading him back there.

She would have pushed him down onto the bed, then let him watch as she slowly stripped down in front of him. He would have loved her pink lace panties and matching bra.

But that was all it could be, a fantasy.

She sat down beside him on a couch, and even though the jets drowned out some of the sound, she could hear his every breath. The sound was mesmerizing, and once again she found herself thinking of more carnal things.

She wasn't some love-struck teenager, but for some reason, whenever she was around him it seemed like she was reverting to her old ways—make love first and ask questions later. But that couldn't be who she was anymore. She was a pro-fessional woman, and as a professional she had to consider more than just her feelings when making a decision, especially when it came to her heart.

His hand rested between them, and she kept glancing down as she wondered how it would feel to take his hand. Now, in this place and nearly alone, she would revel in his touch and the rough calluses that adorned his skin. He had the hands of a man, with one tough patch just below his naked ring finger and another between his pointer and thumb. Actually, it was the callus of a man who handled firearms—often. Far more than a simple security guard would.

She thought about pressing him for more answers about who he really was, but no matter how many questions she asked, he wasn't the kind of man who would willingly supply her with information. Her only hope to really know him would come with patience and time, neither of which she had in spades.

His phone sounded and he pulled it from his breast pocket. *Hotstuff*—that was the caller.

Unless it was a pizza place, there was only one other explanation—his girlfriend was on the line.

He shot Mindy a look and stood up as he answered the phone. "What's up?" he asked, his tone in direct opposition to the name that had flashed on the screen.

Was it possible that the woman on the other end of the line was his ex? Still, if she was calling it had to mean there were still feelings lingering between them.

A niggle of jealousy crept through her, or maybe it was anger that he could have lied to her. Either way, she wished she had stayed in her seat and closer to the comfort of Anya. She shouldn't have let herself imagine anything with him.

Questions first.

"Are you kidding me?" he said, walking over to the bar and pouring himself a scotch. He took a long swig, emptying the tumbler and refilling it.

The last time she had seen a man drink and talk in that manner was when Daniel had gotten the first phone call about Anya. While the situation with his daughter had ended well, it had been a long journey in getting her to the States and under their care.

Oh goodness, what would she do if Jarrod was learning he was a father?

There may have been an increase in cabin pressure, but she was certain that her heart had just dropped into the soles of her feet.

She thought of Daniel and the moment he'd found out he'd become Anya's primary guardian. He had looked so excited, but he'd also looked just as terrified as Jarrod did now. It wasn't that she would have minded dating a single father… That was fine. But what if this new responsibility—or whatever it was that he was learning—took precedence over a relationship?

Jarrod flopped down across from her on the other side of the plane and dropped his forehead into his hands as he grumbled words into his phone. She wasn't completely sure, but it sounded as though he said something like "I can't believe it." From his tone, they weren't the words of a man who was relieved. Rather, they were the words of a man who had been broken.

Chapter Ten

There were fools, and then there were complete idiots—and he was definitely in the latter group. Why hadn't he seen it before?

Jarrod stared down at the industrial carpet of the plane's floor as he tried to make sense of what Zoey was telling him.

"Chad is going to be okay. The bullet just grazed him." Zoey's voice was soft, completely unlike her usual no-nonsense tone. It only made him feel worse. He'd messed up so completely. He should've taken the kidnapper down when he had had his chance, and instead he let the man go. He should have killed him, right there in the middle of the deli, consequences be damned.

"You can't beat yourself up over this," Zoey continued, almost like she could read his mind. "You didn't know they belonged to the Turkish crew. How could you have? They just as easily could have belonged to the people trying to gun down your new girlfriend."

He jerked, gazing over at Mindy. She was hardly his girlfriend. Zoey was just trying to get a rise out of him.

"Either way, I should've taken him out." He shifted, feeling the cool steel of the gun strapped to his ankle.

Mindy looked at him, questions in her eyes. There was a softness there, and it tore at his soul. Normally, he didn't mind keeping a secret—especially when it came to securing his family's safety and anonymity. However, Mindy was different from most. There was something about her that made him want to draw nearer to her. He wanted to whisper secrets into the wisps of her hair and take solace in her arms.

Maybe that was what made him the biggest idiot of all—any person who believed they could trust a stranger was setting himself up for disappointment.

"Are you going to tell her the truth before you get here?" Zoey asked.

"What do you think I should do?" he asked.

"The fact that you're asking tells me you are already compromised enough when it comes to this woman."

That was exactly what he was—compromised. "That didn't answer my question," he said.

"I've a feeling that you are going to do whatever you want, regardless of what I tell you. So, whatever you decide to tell this woman, just make sure you stay safe." Zoey sighed. "Love you, bro, see you soon." Without waiting for him to answer, Zoey hung up.

Did Zoey know something about Mindy that she wasn't telling him? Was Mindy more than she was pretending to be?

All he really knew about her was that she needed him. Maybe that was what he was attracted to. Perhaps he was reveling in his ability to be the white knight although, in reality, he was exactly the opposite. He was a spy in her life, regardless of how much he wanted to be something else.

"Everything okay?" Mindy asked, standing up and walking over to him.

He opened his legs and took her hands and pulled her closer until she was standing between his knees. He looked up at her, taking in the luscious curves of her lips and the gold flecks at the center of her green eyes. He could get lost in her eyes. In fact, that was exactly what he wanted to do. He didn't want to have to question anything anymore. He just wanted her.

"Everything will be fine," he lied. He doubted everything would be okay, especially if Mindy learned that the man at the music class and the man she had killed in her closet had been sent by his enemies and not hers.

He could only imagine what she would say when she learned they were being attacked on all fronts. Rather than being a safe haven, he was only bringing more danger into her life. In fact, if it hadn't been for his enemies and their attack on his life, Mindy and Anya may well have stayed in the city. They could've just gone on living their life… and eventually heard the news about Daniel.

The thought of her brother's death made his entire body clench.

Every bad thing in Mindy and Anya's life was because of him.

If they ever found out the truth, they would hate him. And he wouldn't blame them.

He was struck by the irony in his situation. On one hand, he wanted to tell her who had been stalking them in the city so she could stop thinking someone was after her. And then on the other hand, he was keeping far worse secrets, though he would have liked to think that the secrets he kept were saving her from heartbreak.

But was he really saving her? Was it within his right to keep the truth from her? Or was all of this a feeble attempt to save himself from having to face the consequences from his own series of mistakes?

"You are lying to me. I know when something is wrong." Mindy squeezed his hands and gave him a sweet smile. "I hope you know you can tell me anything."

He jerked. She couldn't have known what he was thinking—he had a better poker face than that—and yet it was like she could read him. He both hated and loved that about her. Few people in this world seemed to have the ability of really being able to know him just by looking into his eyes, and the fact she seemed able to do so terrified him.

He opened his mouth to speak, then closed it again, unsure of exactly what he should say. He hadn't been this big a mess in a long time. He liked it when his life was cut-and-dried, logical, linear. And yet, here he was, befuddled by the beautiful woman standing between his legs.

"I know there's something going on here that you aren't telling me, and I know it's about a woman." She shifted her weight from one foot to the other, nervous. "I get that relationships can't always be categorized as boyfriend and girlfriend or whatever, but if you're dating somebody, that's okay. I'm cool with it."

Oh, hell. Here he had thought she had seen right through him, but what she was really worried about was whether or not he was emotionally available. He wasn't sure if he was relieved or even more concerned.

"I… No… The woman on the phone, that was

my sister. She just had some new information about what happened back there and the picture I took."

Mindy relaxed visibly and let out a long sigh. Her hand loosened in his, but she didn't let go. "Oh," she giggled, sounding slightly embarrassed. "Sorry. I didn't mean to pry. I guess I just have been hurt by so many guys I always assume the worst."

"Are you telling me you're a train wreck when it comes to relationships?" He laughed, glad to take some of the pressure off him and all of his thoughts.

"Hey, *if*—and I'm not admitting that I am—but, *if* I am, it's because of the men I've been in relationships with." She paused. "There's been more than one ex who had calls like the one you just had. I would be stupid to fall into the same trap. I like to think I've learned a thing or two."

"Wouldn't we all like to think we've learned our lessons? That we will never be hurt again?" he said, but as he spoke he stared out the windows into the steadily darkening sky.

"So, I guess I'm not the only one who's a bit of a train wreck." She reached up and ran her fingers through his hair.

The simple action made his breath catch in his throat. He'd forgotten how good it felt to have someone's fingers twist in his hair. His pulse quickened as she cupped his face with her other hand. "Jarrod, I want you to know that I'm grateful—for everything. You've done so much for me and Anya. And, I promise, no matter what happens, just as you have saved us from getting hurt, I will do my best to keep from hurting you."

Just when he had thought he couldn't feel any more at odds with himself, she had to go and say something so tremendously sweet, and soul crushing. It wouldn't have hurt so much if for just a split second he had thought she hadn't meant it, but from the depth in her gaze and the soft lilt of her words, he knew she meant every syllable.

A flood of thoughts of morality and desire moved through him, and in its wake were dreams of what could be.

He stood up and wrapped her in his arms. This woman, this beautiful person, could be his future. She could be his everything.

He pressed his lips against hers. They were as sweet and all-encompassing as the woman they belonged to. And, as he ran his tongue over their curves, he noted that she still tasted of champagne, and it didn't escape him that its flavor was the epitome of the woman it belonged to. She was refined but complex, full of secrets but then whispering of unarguable truths, and beneath it all there was a sweetness that spoke to years spent perfecting itself. Like the flavor on her lips, she was true perfection.

And damn, he wanted her.

All of her.

If she was a bottle of champagne, he would taste her every drop.

Hell, champagne or not, he would savor every bit of her and their time together.

She took a breath, breaking their kiss without moving her lips away from his. "Jarrod… What about Anya?"

"She's down for the count."

She sighed.

He expected her to tell him that this was wrong, ill-fated, even out of line perhaps, but instead she looked up at him, her eyes vibrant. "Take me to the back," she whispered. Her breath brushed his lips. "I want to feel you, all of you."

He was instantly hard, in fact, painfully so. He ached to take her here, now, on the floor, on the counter. It didn't matter. He couldn't wait.

He lifted her up, and she wrapped her legs around his waist as he carried her to the back bedroom of the plane. She shifted her hips, rounding herself against him and making him impossibly harder. He would have to slow her down, no matter how badly he wanted to rip off her clothes and show her exactly how she made him feel.

Thankfully, the flight attendant had disappeared long ago, but he still checked over his shoulder one more time as he stepped into the bedroom and closed the door behind them. For the next hour, or as long as Anya was napping, Mindy was all his.

She ran her fingers through his hair, wrapping it around her fingers and giving it a pull as she took his lips with hers, the action commanding, even aggressive, and one hell of a turn-on.

He moaned into her mouth, and she rocked against him.

Laying her down on the bed, he moved down between her legs. Rubbing his hand over her, he moved his other hand down her leg and pulled off her shoes. He hadn't noticed until now how red they were, almost like a candy apple...the same color her lips had been when he'd first seen her at the meeting. He dropped the shoes to the floor with a thump and moved to take off her pants.

Covering her was a thin layer of pink lace and nothing more. As badly as he wanted to rip them open and take her, he forced himself to slow down, to take pleasure in unwrapping the gift that she was.

"You are so beautiful," he said, leaning back and taking in the sight of her half-naked body.

"You haven't seen all of me," she said with a self-deprecating chuckle. "Just wait until you see how my jelly rolls." She put her hands on her stomach.

Sure, she wasn't a size two, but that didn't matter to him. If anything, he was glad she wasn't. He wanted a woman who was true to herself, true to the needs of her body, and true in her choice of giving her heart and body to him. He wanted her for her and not some stereotype of perfection that was thrust upon them by the world.

In his eyes, regardless of what she thought, she was perfect.

He undid her buttons, revealing a bra exactly the same color as her panties. She had to have planned that, which meant one of two things, either she was the kind of woman who needed to control her life to such an extent that she always wore matching underwear, or she had hoped that things would advance to where they were right now.

"My, Ms. Kohl," he said with a shocked laugh, "were you planning on taking advantage of me?"

She giggled. "You wish."

"Then what is this?" He ran his fingers over the edge of her bra, grazing her nipple with his fingertip ever so lightly.

She moved into his touch. "So, you think just because a woman wears sexy underwear she must be planning on bedding a man? Sir, you are the one who has problems. Can't a woman just want to feel sexy?"

He laughed. Damn, this woman was a challenge, and he loved every second he spent with her that much more for it. "My apologies. I guess I just hoped—"

"That I wanted you?" she said, finishing his sentence.

"A man can wish."

"Do you really need to wish?" She sat up on her elbow and kissed him as her hand slid down and took hold of him. "I've wanted you since the first moment I laid eyes on you at that meeting."

If he was to be honest with himself, he had wanted her even before that, a longing that started when he became acquainted with her file. Hell, maybe seeing her face was the real reason he had made sure he infiltrated her meeting with the Riksdag all in the name of the CIA.

There were just a handful of moments in his life when he felt there was something that was meant to be, almost fated. Meeting her and finding himself between her thighs was one of them. Though he didn't know how this thing would go, there was no question in his mind that this place—and with her—was exactly where he was supposed to find himself.

He silently thanked the Fates.

His prayer was met with the sound of a twisting door handle and the bang of a locked door that was trying to be forced open.

"Anta," Anya said, her voice muffled only slightly by the thin plastic door. "Anta, I hungry."

Mindy sighed, letting go of him and rolling out from underneath before slipping her pants back on. "One minute, sweetheart. I'm on my way." She gave his shoulder an apologetic squeeze.

Jarrod flopped down on the bed as a surge of adrenaline coursed through him thanks to the guilt and fear of being caught.

He was sure the Fates were laughing at his pain. Hopefully, he and Mindy would get the chance to have the last laugh.

Chapter Eleven

It was nearly midnight when the plane touched down on the tarmac. The asphalt was bumpy and little more than a farmer's field with a strip of asphalt, even though it was the private airfield. After they came to a stop, Anya unclipped her belt and ran toward the cockpit and the pilot. "We here?" she called, her voice so high and full of excitement that Jarrod couldn't help smiling.

"Yep, baby girl, we are here." Jarrod stood up and took her by the hand as she toddled from one foot to the other before tumbling to the floor. He helped her up and held out his hand to Mindy.

She looked tired. Her eyes were dark and her hair was falling loose from the clip she had put it up with. She tried to force it to submit as they made their way down the stairs.

There was a black sedan waiting for them and it took them straight to the ranch. As they got out of the car, Zoey stepped outside the main house and waved.

"How was your flight?" she asked.

Mindy flashed Jarrod a guilty smile. "It was good, but it got a little rough about midflight."

He checked his laugh. Zoey would already be looking for something in their relationship to pick apart, and he didn't want to even hint about what had happened—or rather, *hadn't* happened—back on the flight.

He didn't need Zoey questioning his judgment. He was the head of both the family and the STEALTH team, even if Zoey constantly took it upon herself to put him to the test. Though she was his junior, she always seemed to be at odds with him, like somehow it was his fault that she was the youngest.

In a way, Mindy was a bit like Zoey. They were both incredibly strong willed and among the most determined women he had ever met. Hopefully, they would get along.

And hopefully his secret role in Mindy's life wouldn't yet come to light and put their budding relationship in jeopardy.

Zoey opened the back door to the car. "Hiya, little one," she said, giving Anya a high five as Jarrod got her out of her car seat. She introduced herself to Mindy with a handshake. So far, so good.

Anya wiggled in his arms as Zoey stretched her

arms to take the girl. Anya, the girl to whom few were considered strangers, pushed him and motioned for him to let her down. She made her way over to Zoey and wrapped herself around her legs in the smallest bear hug he'd ever seen.

Zoey laughed as she hugged the girl. She motioned them inside. "We have everything ready for you guys. We don't have much in the way of furnishings in the house, but what we do have is yours. So make yourselves comfortable," she said, giving Mindy a little nod.

Maybe his sister had grown up a bit since he had last seen her. Or maybe she was feeling the weight of Trish's loss. Trish had always been the glue that had held the family together and the one to call Jarrod and Zoey to the table when they were at each other's throats.

However, he would do anything for Zoey and she the same for him. And, if anything, her constant pressure had only forced him to work that much harder and for that, they had all benefited.

Mindy took Anya by the hand, pulling her from Zoey's legs and lifting her into her arms. "This little one got a nap, but it is well past her bedtime. Is there anywhere specifically that you would like for her to sleep?" Mindy smiled.

Zoey pointed up the stairs. "Up there, third door down the hall. I made up a bed for both of you.

There's an attached bathroom with everything you need to wash up."

Wow, his sister really had thought of everything.

With a thank-you, Mindy and Anya made their way upstairs. As soon as they turned the corner to the hall and were out of view, Zoey turned on him. "How much does she know? Did you tell her about STEALTH?"

"I haven't told her about us—or anything else. I was hoping that we could get this all sorted with the Riksdag first. I don't want to overwhelm her with everything all at one time."

"That's a cop-out and you know it. You aren't giving this woman enough credit. She is going to figure out what's going on, and then where will you be?" Zoey shook her head. "She has an MBA from Brown—graduating first in her class. She is the type who is going to question the world around her."

"You're right, but what we do shouldn't be on her radar...unless she learns the truth about the kidnapper."

"I'm taking it that you didn't mention his identity to her on the flight?"

He gave her an exasperated look. "Why are you drilling me before I'm even in the house? Can't this wait until morning?"

"You are seriously going to come at me just because I want a little information? I'm helping you, remember?" Zoey rebuked.

He sighed. "Sorry, I'm just tired. It's been a hellish couple of days."

"Apology accepted." Zoey started upstairs, Jarrod close on her heels. "And for now, I'll let Chad and Trevor know where we stand."

"How is Chad doing?" Jarrod asked.

Zoey waved him off. "He's fine. You know Chad—he's tougher than nails and the wound wasn't too bad."

"Sounds like he got lucky," Jarrod said, giving a relieved sigh.

He considered telling Mindy the truth about who he and his family were—it wasn't too late to share some of the truths about STEALTH and his role in her life. But he feared opening up. She was smart. She was going to ask questions, and those questions would only lead to catastrophe.

For now, all he could do was avert disaster and keep anyone else from getting shot. If his family came under fire again, he doubted they would be lucky enough to stay alive.

MINDY ROLLED OVER in the bed and glanced at the clock. It was early but sunlight was starting to creep in. Her body, still on New York time, screamed for her to rise and get to the business of her day. Without a doubt, she had probably missed at least a few hundred emails, most of them urgent, thanks to the loss of her phone.

No wonder she hadn't missed the dang thing.

Getting up, she was careful to not rustle too much. Anya was still asleep on the bed beside her. It had been a long, fitful night for them both. Sleeping next to a child was a bit like sharing a bed with a fish out of water. Anya, though she had been completely asleep, flipped and flung her body around in her ever-pressing need to get comfortable.

As Mindy slipped from the room, her lower back pinged where Anya's wayward foot had found her a few hours earlier. Coffee. Ibuprofen. Phone. And back to work. Just because she had been out of the loop for the last few days didn't mean that the world had stopped. And with Daniel being MIA, she could only imagine the state of things at H&K. There had to be someone available to run the ship.

She made her way down the hall, walking by an open bedroom door. Inside, Jarrod was asleep. He was sprawled out on the bed, taking up nearly the entire thing, and he reminded her of her fight for space with the little fish. He was definitely a man who spent most of his nights alone in his bed. The thought made her smile.

For a second, she considered going into his room, getting into bed with him and finishing what they had started last night, but instead she simply closed his door. What had happened last night on the plane, while fun, had been a bad idea. With sharing bodies came sharing hearts, and hers was already a hot mess.

She needed to get her life back in order and under control before she would be ready to open herself up to what a physical relationship would entail. Even before the last few days, starting a relationship would have been questionable at best. Now, thoughts of starting a relationship were completely asinine.

Her focus had to be on removing herself and Anya from the crosshairs, and then she needed to resolve the obstacles preventing her plants from opening up in Sweden. Until that happened every day was a money-losing day for the company. When Daniel found out, he was going to be furious that she hadn't done her best to watch the bottom line.

Though, thinking about it, he'd be one hell of a hypocrite if he dared to call her out when he'd failed to tell her where he had gone and why. Actually, when he came back, she was going to make it a point to give him a piece of her mind.

Making her way to the kitchen, she found Zoey sitting at the table, tapping away on her computer. "Oh," she said, "good morning. Is it okay if I get some coffee going?" she asked, pointing at the empty coffeepot on the nearly barren kitchen counter.

"Hey," Zoey said, looking up from the screen. Her eyes were red and tired looking, making Mindy wonder if she had even bothered to go to bed the night before. "Go for it. Or if you want, I can do it." Zoey moved to stand up, but Mindy stopped her with a wave of the hand.

"You stay there. I'll grab you up a cup, too." She walked over and started to fill the carafe. "Did you get any sleep last night?"

Zoey shook her head and clicked off her computer before Mindy had a chance to take a good look at whatever was on the screen. The way she moved made her wonder if Zoey was hiding something.

Jarrod hadn't talked about his family very much and, until now, she hadn't really thought to ask much about them. She tried to quell the anxiety and distrust that moved through her as she made the coffee. Zoey was helping with the investigation— nothing more.

Zoey slipped her computer into the case by her feet. She started to stand up, but then stopped herself and reached back into her case. "Hey, I have something for you." She pulled out a phone and handed it to Mindy. "Jarrod said something about you losing yours, so I updated my old one and set it up for you. It's not much, but it will get you through until you're back in the city."

"Wow. I…uh, thank you," Mindy said, taking the phone from Jarrod's sister and clicking it on. It was almost identical to her old one. As she scrolled through it, she was struck by how much Zoey seemed to know about her, though—admittedly—the phone thing might have just been a coincidence. "I appreciate you doing this… I thought I was going to have to hunt down a new one out here in the middle of nowhere."

Zoey laughed, the sound loud and reverberating through the seventies-style kitchen and over the percolating sounds of the coffee maker that was likely from the same era. "I figured as much. You'd almost have better luck finding gold than finding a good smartphone out here." She grabbed two cups from the cupboard and poured them each a mug of the only half-brewed coffee. "You should have seen me when we first got out here. I thought I had found the actual middle of Nowhere, America."

Mindy laughed. "It's a far cry from the city. I'm not gonna lie, I don't think I've ever heard crickets that loud before. Even with the windows closed in our bedroom it sounded like they were in the room with us."

"Knowing this place, they may well have been." Zoey gave her an apologetic smile, as if their home was a poor comparison to what she'd been used to in the city.

"That's not what I meant at all… I guess I'm just not a country girl. I like the amenities that come with city life—constant sirens and all." She took a sip of her coffee, strong and bitter.

"I bet you are thinking about espresso at this very minute. I know I am." Zoey laughed.

She feigned ignorance as she buried her face in her mug and suffered through the next drink of the boiling hot road tar. "I guess making coffee should be put on my list of skills that need a little more work." She reached over for Zoey's cup, but the woman pulled it away.

"No, I don't mind a hearty cup of coffee. In fact, when we've been working overseas there are times when I would give my left leg for even this."

"What is it that you do?" she asked.

Zoey's face tightened. "Well, I've been in the investments game for a long time. Once in a while I travel around and look into whatever our next investment will be, as well as checking my current ones."

Though Zoey's answer made sense, something about it rang false, and she was once again reminded to check her cynicism.

"What kind of things do you invest in?" She knew she should drop the subject, but at the same time she just had to stir the pot and get to the bottom of why she was feeling suspicious.

"This and that," Zoey said, giving a vague wave.

"Jarrod said that you are a genius when it comes to tech. Have you been following everything with Elon Musk?" she asked, trying to make conversation and go a little bit deeper with the woman.

Zoey nodded. "He's an interesting man, but I tend to steer clear of his promises. Though, years or so ago, I went to one of his dinners in Hollywood when he was looking for investors in his latest project. That turned out to be PayPal. So as many successes as I have had, I've had just as many failures and missed opportunities."

"Can you imagine how much those stocks would be worth now?" Mindy asked.

"Millions. That was, if we had played it right. But investing is a gamble. What works for one may not work for another. I mean just look at the Bitcoin boom some time ago. Our company made a substantial profit, but others we know lost nearly everything they had and had to start over. Most of the time, we've been lucky."

"Is that why you all moved here—you got lucky?" Mindy sat down at the table as Zoey stood up, walked over to the counter and poured a bit of sugar into her coffee.

"Yeah, that and a few other reasons." Zoey's face was again pinched, but Mindy wasn't sure if it was from the coffee or from something else. "Did Jarrod tell you about Trish?"

She shook her head.

"Oh," Zoey said, staring into her cup. She took a long breath. "Trish is our sister. She died. A few months ago. It's been hard on the family."

"I... I'm so sorry." Mindy tried to not feel hurt that he had kept a secret so big from her. And on the heels of that was a twang of pity. Here she had been so consumed with her life's upheavals that she hadn't paused for a moment to consider he had things going on in his private life, as well.

Zoey shrugged, but she could tell from the look in Zoey's eyes that it pained to even mention her sister's name. They must have been close.

The door to the kitchen opened and Jarrod walked in. There was a sleepiness to him and his eyes looked heavy. "Hey," he said, walking over to the pot of coffee and pouring himself a cup. "I thought I heard someone talking down here." He glanced over at her and gave her a tired, sexy grin that reminded her entirely too much of their time together on the plane. Her cheeks warmed.

"You hungry? I think there are some frozen waffles or something." Zoey motioned for him to help himself.

"What, no breakfast feast this morning?" he teased.

Zoey gave him a look. "You know how to cook. Feel free to make yourself at home."

"Oh, come on now, sis, you know you want to make me breakfast."

Mindy stood up. "I can make myself useful and start breakfast if you like. It's the least I can do for your generosity in having me here."

Jarrod's smile disappeared, and there was a strange look on his face as he turned to his sister. Zoey cocked her head, quickly glancing between them like she was trying to understand why Mindy would offer to be so nice.

"Seriously, it would be my pleasure. I don't want to impose, and if this is a way I can make your lives easier—"

"No," Zoey said, standing up and walking between her and the stove. "My brother is just kidding around—he knows I hate to cook. Besides, he's lucky that he isn't eating expired MREs while holed up in a cave somewhere. He should consider himself lucky." She glared at him, but there was a faint smile playing across her lips. She walked to the freezer, pulled out a box of Eggos and threw them at him. "Here. Now, stop your whining."

Nearly dropping his cup, he caught the box as it hit him in the ribs.

"While you're at it, why don't you whip up a couple extra for me and Ms. Kohl. We have business to discuss." Zoey grabbed her phone and clicked it on.

"Did you find something?" Jarrod asked.

"Actually, we may have," she said with an excited grin. "The sourcing came back on the chemical samples you sent me from the attack."

A black hole formed in the center of Mindy's chest. She was desperate to hear who may have been behind the attack on Hans, but at the same time, she wasn't entirely sure she was ready. As soon as they located the source and found out who was responsible everything was going to change. It was possible that Jarrod would even leave her here. He had no reason to stay with her and Anya now that she was tucked into the safe harbor of his family's ranch. He was definitely the kind of man who was more comfortable traipsing around the world on a moment's notice than sticking to one place.

Not to mention what it would do for her professionally and personally if her company or her brother had something to do with the attack. Their futures might well be in jeopardy. Not only would their business with Sweden be deemed out of the question, she could easily find herself on the fast track to prison.

But Daniel couldn't have had anything to do with the attack. He would never have ordered such a thing. He wasn't the type. And he certainly wouldn't have done something so rash and put her in danger. That is, unless he was tired of having her at the company. What if he wanted it for himself? As of now, they were profit sharing. Sure, they were both making a decent amount of money, but with her out of the picture he would be making millions more. And he had Anya to support now… Maybe he felt he needed that extra income.

She tried to calm herself and put those kinds of thoughts out of her mind. Her brother didn't hate her. Sure, they weren't the closest of siblings, but for half brother and sister they were certainly a lot closer than most. But then again, Daniel was all business. He was always about the bottom line and how to put more money into his pocket.

Jarrod walked over to her like he could somehow sense her turmoil. "You okay?" he asked, leading her out of the kitchen and away from his sister. "Why don't you just sit down out here on the couch? Let me talk to Zoey for a while, unless you want to come along?" He sat a plate of waffles down on the table in front of her.

"No," she said, shaking her head. "I'm fine. Just…" She didn't know exactly what to say to convey her true feelings of terror and uncertainty. "I need to take a break, maybe get some work done."

"Okay, babe. But know that I get what you're feeling. You've been through a lot in the last couple of days. But everything is going to be okay. You have me." He walked her over to the couch and flicked on the television to some stupid early-morning talk show and handed her the remote. "If you want, just take a break. Veg out for a bit."

As he smiled, relief moved through her. Yes, for the first time in years, she finally felt as though there was someone she could trust.

Chapter Twelve

Jarrod could kick himself for the charade he was being forced to play with Mindy. He made his way to the kitchen, looking back one more time to make sure that she was settled on the couch.

She trusted him.

Hell, from the look she had just given him, her feelings had developed past the almost one-night stand. He might have imagined it, but he could almost have sworn that he saw genuine emotion in her eyes.

For her sake, he was going to have to nip that in the bud. Nearly sleeping with her on the plane had been one heck of a mistake—one he couldn't repeat, no matter how much he wanted to take her in his arms and bed her.

He grabbed his mug and stood in front of the sink, taking a long drink as he remembered how sweet Mindy's lips had tasted. If only he had been able to taste all of her.

"How long have you loved each other?" Zoey asked. "Is this a new development or would you say that you loved her from the first time you laid eyes on her?"

"Zoe, you can be a real pain in the ass sometimes. Did anyone ever tell you that?" he asked, turning to face his sister.

"You. And all the time." Zoey picked up the waffles and returned them to the freezer. "So, really, is this thing you have going with Mindy going to cause a problem with your work? If it is, then maybe it's best if you let me get the truth out of her and you can nose around her company. You know our handlers at the CIA aren't going to patiently wait around for answers, especially once they find out that you are screwing the biggest lead in their case."

"Knock it off, Zoey. You don't know what you're talking about. We haven't *screwed*. We won't *screw*. And if we did *screw* it would be none of your business." He spit the words like they tasted as pithy and dismissive as they sounded.

"Actually, it is my business, Jarrod. It's *all* of our business. If you don't fly straight with the CIA, it's going to affect us all. They are working overtime, just like I am, to get us out of the Gray Wolves' sights. You can't risk pissing them off. If Bayural finds us, we are as good as dead. We have to show the director that we are up to whatever task they give us. And that *you* can keep your pants on."

His sister had a point about their connections within the CIA, but that didn't mean that she had any right to treat him like this. He was the head of this family, not her, no matter how badly she wanted to take the helm. He wasn't stupid and he surely didn't need her treating him like an idiot. At the same time, there was no use picking a fight with her nearly the second he came home. She was just making a show of her role in the family, nothing more. In a few weeks, they would be back into the swing of things and working together in a way that suited them both.

"You just worry about you." He dumped the rest of his coffee in the sink, letting the bitter contents swirl down the drain. He had enough of a burning in his gut. The last thing he needed to do was throw a little battery acid on top of it. "About the nerve agent attack, what did you find out?"

She walked over to the kitchen door and peeked out, checking on Mindy and making sure that she was still watching television. "It looks as though they used a nerve agent called VX. It was the same one that killed the North Korean leader's brother. But this time the attackers chose to turn it into a powder form—and that was likely the only reason you both survived. Had they made it into an aerosol, there is nearly a one-hundred-percent chance that you and Mindy would have never walked away."

"Then I guess it's good that I'm lucky," he said, trying to make light of the attack.

"Yeah, right. That, or the people who threw it weren't looking to kill en masse, rather just a few targets."

"If that was the case, why didn't they just shoot them? Or take care of Hans in his hotel room?"

"My best guess is that they may well have been trying to send your girl, and maybe you, a message. It's more than possible," she said, coming closer so that she could whisper to him, "that this could be somehow connected to our enemies in Turkey. Maybe it was a quick hit by an offshoot gang from the city. Maybe it was just a screwed-up attack. Maybe they meant to go after you and thought they were close enough. Maybe it was supposed to send a message to our family."

"I thought you said you had answers. If I wanted to have everything even further up in the air, I could have taken this all to Chad and Trevor."

"Hey, jerk." Zoey punched him in the arm with a little laugh. Finally they were making some sort of progress with one another, even if it came off as ribbing. "There is more. As far as the sourcing, like I said, we got a manufacturing point. In fact, based on the strontium levels contained within the source compounds, it appears this batch was made in North Korea."

Turkey and North Korea had well-known ties within the black market, and there had been whispers that there was a secret armistice between the two opposing governments that made them common enemies of the United States, whispers that he knew to be true. Which meant he very well may have been the target in the nerve agent attack and that perhaps this had nothing to do with Mindy and Daniel as he had previously assumed.

It only made him feel more like scum.

MINDY CLICKED ON her phone and entered the passwords required to sync her account. As of this morning, she had close to seven hundred emails that had piled up since she had been gone. While most of them could wait, there were plenty that needed her approval or insight. She moved down the list, approving everything from compliance statements to work orders that had defaulted thanks to her brother's absence.

Maybe she had made a mistake in coming to Montana. Maybe she and Anya would have been better off holing up in one of her factories on the West Coast, taking in the warm fall weather on the southern California coastline.

Then again, there was no way she would have refused Jarrod's offer to bring them here. He could have asked her to go to the moon and she would have followed him.

She would have to work on that…at some point.

There was a press release about Hans's death. From the Riksdag's letter, it appeared that there would be a private service for the man, and a public memorial would take place next week. If the situation was different, and her safety wasn't in question, she would have flown to Sweden in order to pay respects to the man and his family. It was the least she could have done, though they weren't exactly what she called allies.

The man, though he had impeded her company's progress, hadn't deserved to die—and certainly not as he had.

She emailed her personal assistant, telling him to send flowers.

Near the bottom of her monstrous inbox, she nearly missed it, but there was an email from Daniel. It didn't have a subject line.

Thank goodness, you're all right, she thought. *At least I can put some of my fears to rest.*

She clicked it open.

A video started to play.

It was all over the place and she could hear voices yelling in English, but the sound was garbled as though someone had a hand over the phone's mic.

Her brother's face flashed on the screen. His

dark eyes were filled with terror. He was wearing his business suit. The phone fell, scanning over carpet, carpet that matched that found in their offices in Washington, DC. The screen went black.

Daniel yelled. "What in the hell are you doing? Why are you arresting me?"

"Put your hands behind your back!" a man ordered.

"Where's your warrant?" Daniel called.

The camera jerked, and a man's black wing tip shoes came into the screen. The view shifted again like someone had kicked his phone out of his hand. As the phone skidded over the floor, the video blurry, a face came into view. Standing over the phone, his face stoic and emotionless, was Jarrod.

Chapter Thirteen

She was numb. Though she should be angry, hurt or confused, she felt nothing. Or maybe it was just that she felt everything all at once. Maybe it was shock.

Yes, shock.

Or maybe she was dreaming. There's no way that could have been Jarrod standing over her brother during his arrest. Jarrod wouldn't—no, *couldn't*—have kept a secret like this from her for so long.

Maybe he had a twin brother. He'd said something about his brothers. But as she thought it, she knew she was lying to herself.

Though the mere thought sickened her, she replayed the video. This time, as she watched, tears streamed down her face, dripping onto her chest as if they could somehow mend her shattered heart. If only it was that easy.

She paused the video and zoomed in on Jarrod's

face. There was no mistaking him. There were the blue eyes that only last night had been fixed to her face, his hands that had traced the curves of her body, and the lips that had promised her solace from the storm of her life.

Jarrod had lied to her.

He had betrayed her.

And the entire time he had told her that he was there to protect her, to keep her safe.

She had wanted to give herself to him, this man…this *liar*.

The door to the kitchen opened, and he and his sister walked out. She wanted to scream, to purge all of her anger. Instead, she stared at him and said nothing.

What could she say? There were no words that would fix what he had done or repair her broken trust.

He took one look at her and stopped. Zoey was saying something and seemed unaware that anything was wrong with her brother and the way he was looking at Mindy.

"What happened?" he asked, the words barely above a whisper.

She wanted to take her phone and shove it in his face and make him watch the despicable video. But it would do nothing except give him more time to come up with some excuse.

She would not allow it.

"Where's Daniel?" she asked, sounding far calmer than she felt.

"I don't—" he started.

"Don't you *dare* lie to me." Her words were laced with rage.

He looked over at Zoey as if she could supply him with the answers.

"Answer me, Jarrod."

He glanced back at her, and there was a look of despair in his eyes. She didn't care how he felt. He *should* be sorry. Hell, he should've been *far* more than sorry. He should've lain at her feet, begging for mercy, and instead he had the audacity to try to continue lying to her. She could never forgive him for what he had done to her, for what he was doing to her now.

What a fool she had been.

Then again, perhaps she was foolish only for trusting him. People were forced to trust one another sometimes. Her only mistake was trusting the wrong one.

"I'm so sorry, Mindy." Jarrod moved toward her, but as he advanced, she stood up and backed away.

"Stay where you are. I want you nowhere near me," she said, bitterness dripping through her words.

"I didn't have a choice…" Jarrod said.

Zoey looked between them and left the room

without a word. Her exodus made Mindy wonder if she knew about Jarrod's betrayal. The sting from his actions worsened.

"Who told you?" Jarrod leaned against the couch as though it was the only thing keeping him from falling.

The simple action only angered her further. How dare he be so upset. This was his fault. This was all his doing, yet he seemed almost as shattered and hurt by the revelation as she was.

"Daniel sent me a video while he was being arrested. It was taken during his arrest. You were in the background." She paused. "Don't bother lying to me any longer. I now know exactly who you are—you're my enemy."

Jarrod sat heavily on the arm of the couch. "Mindy, please don't think that. I promise I never wanted you to get hurt. I only wanted to help you. I wanted to clear your name." He paused. "I never wanted Daniel to die."

Holy crap.

What was he talking about? She sat on the fireplace hearth, folding her knees to her chest.

Daniel is dead.

She dropped her head to her knees as she realized that she had forgotten how to breathe.

Daniel was her lifeline. He was her everything. He was the only family she had left.

Except Anya.

And what about Anya?

Who would care for her now, now that he was *dead*? The word rattled through her like a cascade of marbles falling through a steel grate.

Breathe in.

The oxygen tore at her air-stricken lungs, making them burn, but the pain was nothing compared to the agony of this new revelation.

Jarrod had a role not only in her brother's arrest but also in his death. It was too much to bear.

How could Jarrod even dare to look her in the eyes this entire time?

Once again, she found herself filled with questions, and she had no idea where to begin in order to get the answers she needed.

Moreover, she wasn't sure that she could handle more bad news. One more heartbreak and she would likely meet her own death, as well.

There was a tickle upon her cheek, and she realized that she was crying. She bit her cheek, hoping to stanch her tears. Jarrod had no right to see her at her weakest. He didn't deserve to share in any of her emotions. He deserved to go straight to hell.

She wiped the tears from her face. The most important question she could think of slipped from her lips. "Why?"

"I didn't want him to die because—"

"No," she said, trying to read the truth or a lie in his face. "Why did you kill him?"

"My God, no…" Jarrod stammered. "I didn't… I didn't kill your brother."

He couldn't expect her to believe him. Not after what she'd just seen. "Don't lie to me, Jarrod. At least treat me with some amount of respect after everything you've done."

He shrank in the seat. "Mindy, I think you have this all wrong. I didn't kill your brother. I don't wish you any ill will. And I know you probably don't think you can trust me right now, but I swear to you that I'm on your side."

She didn't know exactly what he meant when he said he was on her side, and right now she didn't even want to ask. No doubt, he would simply feed her some other rehearsed line.

"I know nothing about you. You and your supposed family, you all may be putting me on." She checked the tears that once again threatened to fall. "I want… No, I *have* to get out of here." She stood up and walked to the window, turning her back on him to hide another wave of tears.

She couldn't be weak, not now, not when she was so vulnerable.

"Mindy, no." Jarrod moved closer, stopping beside her. "You don't have to leave. At least let me explain myself about what is going on. Then, if you like, you can go. I will even drive you to the airport and get you a private jet home. I swear." There was a softness to his voice that made her want to fall into his arms even though he was her enemy. She just needed someone she could trust implicitly. Someone who would hold her right now and tell her that everything was going to be okay.

But she couldn't fall into the trap that was Jarrod Martin.

"If you didn't kill my brother, then who did?"

"Your brother's death was an unfortunate accident." Jarrod sighed. "We were questioning him and my colleague misread the situation. He thought your brother was holding a weapon and he was forced to act."

"Forced to act?" she repeated, chuckling at the macabre absurdity of his words. "First, who are you really? Is everything you've told me before now been a lie? Is your name even Jarrod?"

"My name really is Jarrod. And all the feelings that I've had for you are real. I meant everything I said to you."

"You just omitted some key details." She turned to face him, new rage filling her. "You can't possibly believe you're worthy of my trust."

She could see her words strike a nerve.

"I… I know," he said, sounding as broken as she felt. "I hate myself for what I have been forced to keep from you. When I took this job, I thought I could keep my feelings for you at bay. But you're unlike anyone I've ever had to work with before."

She couldn't listen to his words. If she did, they

had the power to break her heart. "*Work with?* Doing what?"

He hesitated for a moment, as though trying to decide whether to tell her the truth. She glared at him and his reticence seemed to wither away.

"My family and I are also business owners, but our business is slightly different from yours. We own and manage a company called STEALTH. We're independent military contractors, and—"

"You are *mercenaries*?" What did mercenaries have to do with her brother?

What had Daniel been doing?

"We're not mercenaries, we're contractors—an entirely different thing."

"Do you kill people in the name of the United States government?" she asked, trying to make sense of what he was telling her.

"On occasion, but that is rarely our mission."

"Okay, you are only mercenaries *on occasion.* Please tell me how that isn't being a mercenary?"

"That isn't all that we do. Like with your brother."

"And yet he ended up dead, strange." Her anger flared.

"In your brother's case, I was there working as a hired contractor, which included interrogating him for the CIA. My background makes me what some would call an interrogation specialist."

"The CIA?" She paused, at a loss. "Why would the CIA want to interrogate Daniel?"

"They had reason to believe he was selling state secrets to foreign governments."

"You thought my brother was a *spy*?" She choked on the word.

He didn't say anything.

A sickening realization welled within her. "Do you think I'm a spy, as well? Is that why you brought me here?" She swallowed back the lump that formed in her throat. "Did you set the whole thing up with Hans? Did you manipulate me into thinking that you were my friend?"

"I am your friend. I am your ally. And no, I didn't have anything to do with Hans's death." He paused. "I have my people within the agencies looking into the attack. The biggest break we have had so far was what Zoey just told me about linking the nerve gas to North Korea."

She was so confused. He still hadn't told her whether she was under investigation by the CIA. And somehow they had ties to North Korea? What had happened to her almost-boring life?

"What does all of this have to do with me and my family?" She stopped for a moment. "Was Daniel selling secrets to North Korea?" The implications nearly brought her to her knees.

Daniel wouldn't do this kind of thing. He'd only been the head of the company for a year now. He couldn't have gotten himself in this much trouble so quickly—or could he? What had Daniel been doing behind her back?

The thought of her brother and Jarrod betraying her… She really had no one.

If only she could reach out to Daniel and ask him what he had done. And why.

How could he have gone against the family when he had a child who depended on him?

She reminded herself to breathe. This was it. She was going to have a full-blown panic attack.

There was a deep pain in her chest, and she could swear that her arms were numb.

Her vision tunneled and blurred.

Then her world went black.

Chapter Fourteen

"So, you finally had to tell her?" Zoey said with a pitying look on her face as she rushed into the room, no doubt flushed out of hiding by the sound of Mindy hitting the ground.

He knelt beside Mindy and pushed her hair back from her face. There was a thin sheen of sweat on her forehead and her pulse was rapid, but he was sure she was going to be okay. Or at least that she would wake up.

"And I'm guessing, based on the state of your girlfriend, that it didn't go quite as well as you were hoping?" Zoey continued.

Mindy started to blink, but she didn't seem to be focusing on anything in particular as she struggled to regain her bearings.

"Be quiet, Zoey," he said, lifting Mindy into his arms with an *oomph*. "I don't need your judgment right now."

Mindy rolled into him, her head against his

neck. "You're going to be all right. I've got you," he cooed.

Mindy answered with a weak nod.

"I heard you telling her about STEALTH. Do you really think that was your place?" Zoey continued on her rampage.

He stared daggers at his sister. "You told me to tell her whatever I thought was necessary. It was goddamned necessary that she knew that I'm on her side…that I didn't want her or her brother to get hurt."

"And yet here we are." Zoey motioned toward Mindy. "Don't you think you should leave the poor woman alone? Let someone else handle this investigation?"

Damn Zoey for putting him on the spot. And damn her for being right. Damn it all.

"Do you want to take this over? Were you in the room with Daniel?" He seethed. "I know you think you have all the answers. I know you think you're smarter than me, but until you know everything, and until you feel what I'm feeling, just be quiet and get out of my way." He pushed past her as he made his way down the hall and to the stairwell. He carried Mindy up the stairs, nearly running away from his sister.

As he made it to the upstairs hall, Anya came walking out of her room. She was rubbing her eyes. Before she had the chance to see him and the state her aunt was in, he ducked into the nearest bedroom—his own.

He closed the door quietly behind them with his foot. Hopefully, Mindy wouldn't be furious to find herself in his room. She was already having a hard enough time trying to work through everything. It was really no wonder that she had fainted.

There was the sound of Anya humming in the hallway. She sounded sleepy and she grew louder as she came near his door. She stopped and walked into the bathroom that was nearest them. From the sound of her singing, he could tell she hadn't bothered to close the bathroom door as she went to her business.

Mindy was growing heavy in his arms. His biceps burned as he held her, unsure of whether to take her to her own bed or simply put her down in his bed and hope for the best. So far, hoping for the best had been biting him in the ass.

His shoulders ached.

He gently laid her on his bed. It would be easier to explain to her than to Anya. He could almost imagine Anya and her questions now. No doubt there would be questions about their friendship.

He pulled a blanket over Mindy and tucked it gently under her arms before making his way out and into the hallway. Anya was just walking out of the bathroom.

"Good morning, sweetheart," he said, trying

to sound like his world and his hopes for the future weren't crashing down around him. "Did you sleep well?"

"Uh-huh," Anya said, looking up at him with her big sleepy eyes.

There was the sound of footsteps ascending the staircase, and Zoey made her way onto the landing. Taking one look at them, she smiled. "Hiya, big girl, are you hungry?" She stuck out her hand. "How about I take you downstairs and rustle us up something to eat while Jarrod gets ready for the day."

"I want Anta," Anya said, looking around.

"She's taking a nap, sweetheart," Zoey said, moving closer and taking the little girl's hand. "Let's let her sleep a bit more before we wake her up. After your big, long flight last night, I bet she's tired. Do you want to tell me about your plane ride? Did you have fun?" She pulled the little girl up into her arms as she started to make their way toward the stairs. She looked back at Jarrod and mouthed the words *I'm sorry*.

The only thing his sister had to be sorry about was that she hadn't stopped them from getting into this predicament. Yet, even if she had spoken out against him taking this job, he was sure he wouldn't have listened. When it came to his feelings and how he acted upon them, he would never be more than a fool.

He walked into the bathroom, grabbed a wash-cloth and wet it. Mindy was still on the bed and her eyes were closed. Part of him wondered if she had woken while he had been in the hall and was now faking being unconscious just so she didn't have to face him.

He wouldn't have blamed her.

If only she understood he was simply doing his job, and he had only brought her here to keep her safe. He had really been acting out of what he had believed were his best intentions—though, look-ing back, part of the reason he had wanted to keep her safe and out of harm's reach was because he was falling for her.

And look where those damn feelings had landed them.

He sat beside her on the bed and ran the cool cloth over her brow. She stirred a bit at the chill, but her eyes remained closed.

She wasn't faking it, but she clearly wasn't in a damned hurry to come back to him.

There was the buzz of her phone from her pocket.

It buzzed again.

He had been behind Zoey giving her the phone and getting her access to work, but he was sur-prised that people were already trying to get ahold of her. He looked down at his watch. Then again, they were on Eastern Time. Though it was early morning in Montana, it was late morning there. And she probably hadn't told anyone where she had gone. At least, he hoped she hadn't.

His family's secret popped into his mind. If Mindy had notified someone that she was here, and revealed who she was with, it would put his entire family at risk of being found by the Gray Wolves. If the organization heard even a whisper of where they might be, they would descend upon them.

It was all his fault.

If only he could go back in time and turn down this job. If only he could have faced Trish's loss and the family's grief instead of running and hiding himself behind the emotional walls of his work, it would have saved them all a great deal of heartache.

Then again, he would have never met Mindy.

Even if things weren't turning out as he had hoped, at least they'd had one wonderful night together. Though they hadn't completely given themselves to one another, it was still one of those nights that he would hold on to forever. Sometimes the preamble to making love was even more exhilarating than the act itself. If they had gone all the way, and if it was impossibly better than the moments they had shared, he would probably have died from ecstasy.

Her phone buzzed again, sounding even more insistent.

Reaching down, and careful not to invade her privacy, he pulled the phone from the pocket of her sweater.

There, on the screen, was the name Arthur.

His first thoughts were of the rookie that had taken Daniel down. He laughed at his reaction. Agent Arthur wasn't actively pursuing this lead. And, if he was, Jarrod's handlers at the CIA would have told him.

And he doubted that Agent Arthur was the kind who would go behind his superior's backs, at least not this early in his career. Something like that, disobeying orders, would get him sent straight back to the civilian world.

Still, he couldn't shake his illogical fear.

What if Mindy had been playing him instead of the other way around? What if she had known about Daniel's death the entire time and had just been using him so that she could come here and infiltrate his family for the Gray Wolves? What if she was here to kill him and his family?

What if he had set a Wolf loose in their home?

He stood up from the bed as he stuffed Mindy's new phone into his pocket.

Mindy moaned from the bed and her eyes fluttered open.

He wasn't sure what to do. There she was, lying in front of him, her pink lips parted as though she was waiting for his kiss.

For the first time, he realized that this confusion, this complete loss of bearings, must be exactly what she was feeling, as well. That is, if she wasn't a spy for the Gray Wolves.

She moaned again, and this time it carried the soft hoarseness of one who had just made love. The sound pierced the feeble shell he had been trying to build around himself.

There was no way she could have faked this. She had been taken to her knees by his revelation.

He couldn't project his guilt onto her. No. He was the one who had made mistakes.

He knew he was trying to rationalize, but he couldn't have told her who he was before or his role in her brother's death. No. He had done what he had to do. Being covert was as much a part of his job as meetings with dignitaries and the like was a part of hers.

His anger surprised him. He tried to stanch it, but the more he thought of his justifications, the angrier he became. It wasn't just anger with her, but rather the entire situation.

Mindy opened her eyes. He knelt down. "Why don't you stay here and rest. I'll come up and check on you in a little bit. In the meantime, I'm going to go and make sure that Anya has breakfast."

Mindy moved to argue, but as she sat up, she was taken with what he assumed was another feeling of faintness.

"Just rest. When you feel better, we can talk," he said, trying to keep his tone neutral.

She nodded and laid her head back on his pillow.

As he closed the door behind him, he couldn't help feeling thankful that for once a woman in his life hadn't argued with him.

He sat down at the top of the stairs, not ready to face his sister. Taking out Mindy's phone, he opened it up using a password he had noticed her using. Luckily, he got it right on his first try.

On the home screen were the icons for her email as well as the notification that she had missed a call. He needed to be careful not to leave any tracks of his snooping. If she found out, there was absolutely no way he would ever get back into her good graces. As it was, there was only a slight chance of reconciliation between them.

Opening up the phone icon, he scrolled through her call log.

Picking through the numbers, he tried to see if he recognized any, but none stood out. He turned to his own phone and looked up Agent Arthur's cell. Out of curiosity and a desperate hope he was wrong, he did a search for the number. Nothing came up.

He felt a bit of relief in finding out that his fears about her double-crossing him were completely unfounded, but there was still something nagging him that he couldn't quite put his finger on.

Mindy hadn't seemed like the type who would play him, at least not intentionally.

On the heels of that thought was the realization that he was being a hypocrite.

Even if she was working against him, how could he begrudge her—what if she was only doing her job?

No. She wasn't working against him.

He just needed to make things right between them, and make her understand his actions. Then, perhaps, they could go back to where they once were, lying in each other's arms and whispering late into the night. She could be his and he could be hers. They could belong to one another forever.

And maybe that was nothing more than a pipe dream, and he had screwed up the only future he had ever truly hoped for.

He clicked on her photo album in the cloud, hoping to see a picture of her smiling, anything that could help ease the pain that was filling his heart.

There were dozens of pictures of her and Anya playing in Central Park, one of them on the boardwalk on the Jersey Shore, and another where she was laughing and Anya's face was filled with mischief. In every photo, she and Anya looked sublimely happy. It was almost as if the two of them were only truly happy when they were together.

Which made him wonder... If things did go his way, and they reconciled, would there be any room for him in their little club of two?

From the top of the stairs, he could make out the sweet trills of Anya's voice drifting up to him from the kitchen. The sound was broken by the ting of a metal spoon on a cereal bowl and the echoes of his sister's laugh.

He could see how easy it was to love a girl like Anya. She was the epitome of innocent sweetness. There were no questions about the little girl's thoughts or feelings—she just put them out there without fear of consequence or reprimand.

If adults were the same, life would be easier in so many ways.

He closed his eyes and tried to envision a future with Anya and Mindy. He could almost see them now, sitting downstairs with his family eating breakfast. When they were together, really together, it would become his mission to make a full spread—ham, eggs, potatoes, toast, waffles, pancakes, sausage, bacon and even beans for his brothers Chad and Trevor, who could eat everything in sight. Trevor had always loved when they'd spent time in England and had the chance to gorge themselves on the full fry-ups.

He smiled at the thought of them all together.

Again, the ache for Trish returned.

He couldn't help but wonder if the grief that came with her loss would ever go away.

Anya laughed, the sound bright and cheerful.

What would happen to her when she learned of her father's death? Would she feel the same way he did about Trish? Would his absence from her life be a constant sting, or was Anya still young enough that his loss wouldn't be as hard to deal with as it would have been if the girl was older?

The ache in his chest intensified.

If only he had stopped Agent Arthur from hurting the man. If only he could have seen what was to come.

If only, if only… He had to stop. He had to take control of the situation. It was his only choice. He couldn't stand by and hope time would dull the pain and anguish caused by his mistakes. He had to move forward and do everything in his power to make things right.

Renewed, he stood up and started to walk down the stairs.

Mindy's phone rang in his hand once more.

Again the caller was "Arthur," and the familiar twinge of angst filled him. He ignored the call and sent it to voice mail.

He started to close the photo app, planning to cover his tracks, but as he did, the photo album he'd been looking at flipped to another. There, standing at what looked like a company luncheon, complete with a spread of firearm prototypes of all sizes and colors, was Mindy. Standing behind her, and to her left, was none other than Agent Arthur.

So much for hope, and so much for "if only." Now he was left with one choice alone: to kill or be killed.

Chapter Fifteen

The door to Jarrod's room slammed open, hitting the wall behind it so hard that the door handle stuck in the drywall. "Are you kidding me?" Jarrod said, his voice somewhere between a terrifying yell and a sobering accusation.

Mindy tried to sit up in bed, but as she moved, her head throbbed. "What? What is it?" As she looked up at him, rage and hurt in his eyes, she was brought back to what had happened between them.

"You've been lying to me," he said, pain flecking his voice.

She swung her legs over the edge of the bed, trying to force her body to submit to her will and simply regain her equilibrium. "I don't know why in the hell you're pissed off at me, when I'm the one who has every right to be angry here."

"I admit that I screwed up." He took a long breath as though he was trying to control his temper. "I kept the truth of who I was from you, but I did so for both of our benefits. But how dare you judge me when you're keeping your own secrets from me."

She was at a loss. "What are you talking about, Jarrod?"

He thrust her phone at her. "Why didn't you tell me that you've been working with Agent Arthur?"

She had no idea what he was talking about. "Agent Arthur?"

He clicked on the screen, using a password that she hadn't given him yet he seemed to somehow know. She thought about asking why he thought it was okay to steal her password and invade her privacy, but they were well past that point. Now, as far as she could tell, they were both at a place of all or nothing.

If she hadn't fainted, she had no doubt that he would have had her ass on a plane at that very moment.

"Who is this?" he asked, pulling up a picture of the company's last summit meeting.

There was a large group of people in the photo. When the photo had been taken they were in the middle of reviewing next year's weapon proto-types. They were going to unveil a new line of long-range military-grade rifles.

Her engineers had put a great deal of time and effort in the design. In fact, it was the line they had intended on manufacturing in Sweden.

The thought made her stomach clench as she thought of Hans and the Riksdag. And Daniel.

"Who?" she asked, looking at the many faces of people standing around her in the photo.

He pointed at a tall and muscular man standing behind her in the picture.

"That guy?" she said with a chuckle. "Oh, you are being ridiculous if you are worried about him. That's one of my assistants, Arthur McDuffy."

Jarrod made a strange wheezing sound as he dropped her phone onto the bed beside her. "Did Daniel know him?"

"They might have seen each other, but rarely. Why?"

Jarrod shook his head, saying nothing as he stared down at his toes.

"Now, was there a reason you thought it was okay to go through my things?" She shut off the screen on her phone and slid it under her leg. "If you want, I can go find my purse and let you look into that, as well. Or, you could just ask me about whatever it is that you think I'm guilty of."

He stared vacantly at the place where she had tucked the phone beneath her leg.

"I bet this is just your way of taking the pressure off you. Something you learned in the CIA? You know, the old bait and switch thing? Make me look guilty of some nonsense thing in order to make me think that you aren't the worst kind of man on earth?" As she spoke, anger roiled through her, washing away any remnants of the feebleness she had been feeling. "Well, guess what? You are the one who is in the wrong here. I've done nothing."

She stared at him waiting for a response. He didn't move.

"You asked me to listen to your side of the story, to hear why you did what you did. I get that you didn't think you had a choice, but you know what, Jarrod? I don't forgive you. You lied to me. You played Anya and me for fools. And no matter what comes, or what risks are waiting for us, I want to go back home."

He jerked. "You can't."

"Why? You want me to stay here?" she rebuked, knowing that she was calling him deeper into the fight. She gave a dry, angry chuckle. "You've done nothing but manipulate me. Enough is enough, Jarrod."

"I know you aren't going to listen to me, but I wish you would." He paused. "I didn't bring you here to manipulate you. I just wanted to help."

"You keep telling yourself that," she said, crossing her arms over her chest and protecting what little there was left of her heart.

"You have every right to be angry," he said. When she didn't respond, he continued. "How long have you known McDuffy?" He finally looked her in the eye.

She shrugged. "You aren't about to change the subject on me."

"Just answer me." He wasn't angry, just insistent, which made her come to a screeching halt.

What was he getting at by going after Arthur? And what did it matter?

"I don't know." She thought for a moment. "I guess he's been working for me for about the last six months."

Jarrod turned away from her and slowly paced around the room. "How did he get hired?" Before she could answer, he continued, "Did you run any sort of background check on the man?"

"That kind of thing is my HR team's job, but I'm sure they were done." She paused. "Do you think he had something to do with the nerve agent attack, or something to do with Daniel?"

He snorted like he knew something that she didn't. Her anger rose to the surface once again.

"Look, Jarrod, if we are going to get along… and if you want me to forgive you for lying to me, then you and I are going to have to get something straight. You have to tell me the truth. We have to be honest with one another. Or else, what is the point? I won't be able to trust you and you won't be able to trust me."

As it was, even if he was honest with her, she wasn't sure if she could ever really trust him again.

He had broken her heart into a million pieces. Her trust was completely shattered.

"Let's just say that I know Arthur."

She could have sworn he said something under his breath that she couldn't quite hear.

She sighed. He still wasn't telling her anything. She should have seen him for the interrogation specialist he was. "Arthur formerly worked for my father. He was one of several of his assistants. How do you know him, Jarrod?"

She could have sworn Jarrod's face paled.

"Did he have access to any private information?" he asked.

"Not my files." She nibbled at the corner of her cheek. "At least I don't think so."

"And what about your father's?" he pressed.

She shrugged. "I don't know. It was rare that my father even let my brother and me into his office, let alone have any kind of dealings with the day-to-day running of the company."

"And yet you and your brother were left with the company after your father's death?"

He sounded so judgmental. What was he trying to insinuate?

"Look, I've done the very best I could, given the circumstances of my father's death. I have worked hard to understand and run the company the way he would have wanted." She stood up, readying herself for another battle with the man with whom she had previously shared her bed.

"I'm sorry," he said, taking her hands in his.

She wanted to pull away, but she yearned to feel his touch once again. When he had been with her on the plane, his touch had reawakened a part of her that she had given up hope on.

If he truly didn't have anything to do with her brother's death, and had been merely a bystander as he claimed, then perhaps there was room in her heart for forgiveness.

She may have caught him in a lie, but he didn't have to tell her about his investigation. In divulging the truth to her, he had opened himself up to far-reaching consequences. If the CIA found out that he had acted against their best interest, his job—and maybe even his life—would be in jeopardy.

Not for the first time, she was reminded that he had put his life on the line for her.

But it didn't negate the fact that he'd kept the truth of her brother's death from her.

Still, she didn't pull away from his touch.

"Now, are you going to answer me, Jarrod Martin, or do I need to sit you down on this bed and interrogate you as you have interrogated me?"

His lips formed a smile, like he found what she was saying to be some kind of turn-on instead of the castigation it was intended to be. She considered correcting him, but oh, that smile. She loved that smile.

"Ask away." He let go of her hands and sat down upon the bed.

"How did my brother die?"

"Do you really want to know?" he asked, giving her a look of pity.

"I just need to know if he suffered." The lump returned in her throat.

"No, don't worry, it was quick," Jarrod said, taking hold of her fingers and giving them a reassuring and apologetic squeeze. "During my questioning, the rookie agent, Agent Arthur was there."

"My Arthur?" she asked, some of the faintness she had been feeling threatening to return.

"The one and only." Jarrod nodded. "Your brother moved for something in his pocket and pulled out a pen. Agent Arthur mistook it for a weapon and shot him in the chest. At least that was how it seemed at the time. Now I have to assume he intended to kill him all along."

"What happened to Arthur?" she asked, moving to sit back down on the bed beside Jarrod.

"I'm sure his actions are being investigated by the CIA. Though spooks have a different set of standards, shooting someone in the middle of interrogation isn't something they are going to ignore."

"And you think Arthur was out to murder my brother?" Her words came out as a whisper, like they were some kind of secret that she could barely utter.

"Until I saw that photo, the thought hadn't crossed my mind. But now I'm sure that was his intention." Jarrod reached up and pushed a loose hair behind her ear. "Are you feeling any better?"

She had been until now. Just when she thought her world couldn't be more in turmoil, there was another twist.

"Do you think it was Arthur who was selling our company's secrets to North Korea?"

Jarrod nodded. "Everything seems to be pointing that way. My best guess is that he was compromised by North Korean agents when he worked for your dad. They probably paid him well for his services."

She leaned into him, letting him wrap his arm around her. "Did you try and save my brother?"

He sighed. "There wasn't time. I should have seen Arthur going for his gun, but I missed it. I'm so sorry, babe."

She felt herself soften as he called her by the pet name. Though she was deeply saddened by the loss of Daniel and the lies that were unfolding around them, she didn't have it in her to completely turn Jarrod out. She was angry and hurt, but without him at her side she was left with no one. As it was, she was already more alone than she had ever been. She needed him. And gauging from his rapid heartbeat as she drew closer, she could tell that he needed her, too.

Right now, they were each other's rocks, and the world around them was their hard place.

Chapter Sixteen

Jarrod was at a loss. Although he had finally gotten a break in the case, he was unsure of what to do. If Agent Arthur truly was a double agent for the North Korean government and the CIA, he would be a very dangerous suspect to pursue.

And if he did go after Arthur, he couldn't leave Mindy and Anya in his sister's care. Not when she was here alone. They would be vulnerable to attack. If the Gray Wolves found them, there would be nothing to stop them without him here. Sure, they were tough women…and his sister was one heck of a shot, but he wasn't willing to take the risk.

He also couldn't take Mindy and Anya with him.

What would happen if the North Koreans found out that their agent and source had been revealed? He couldn't know for sure if they would simply let Arthur fall under the hatchet or if they would stop at nothing to prevent him from being taken out. No doubt, if they thought that he and Mindy were the only ones who bore witness to the truth, they would come after them in order to protect their investment.

Jarrod couldn't be certain that Arthur truly belonged to the North Koreans. He would have gone through rigorous background checks and training to become a CIA agent, not to mention his work as an undercover agent within Mindy's company. So, either Jarrod was missing something, or Arthur and his people had someone working for them within the agency.

Of the two, he had a feeling it was the latter.

Double agents, though difficult to identify and pin down, weren't hard to come by. They were much like police officers in the sense that in order to be a good police officer one must also have the mind-set of a great criminal. Only an uncorrupted moral compass set the two apart.

"What are we going to do, Jarrod?" Mindy asked, and as she spoke her body vibrated against his, filling him with a strange sensation of never wanting to be apart from her again.

Giving in to that desire, to keep her at his side always, would only put her in more danger than he already had. And yet, here he was, the one she depended on for answers, and he only had more questions.

"I could go to my people at the CIA, but I'm worried that they may have a leak." He took his phone out from his pocket and sent a text off to Zoey. The sooner she could get to work, the better. They were already behind the eight ball when it came to this investigation. And now, with his concerns about a leak in the agency, STEALTH was the only group he could trust.

Zoey's code name popped up on the screen as she pressed for more information. As quickly as he could, he told her exactly what they knew. She was their greatest weapon when it came to finding out secrets.

"I'll strip him of all of his access. I have some great people on my staff, especially in IT." She smiled up at him. "Your sister isn't the only one with a corner on the hacker market."

He didn't doubt that for a second, but if her people were as good as she thought they were, how in the hell did they miss Arthur stealing secrets in the first place? Still, they could be put to work in the meantime.

"Why don't you call your people. Have them start going through Arthur's computer. See if they can dig up anything that would indicate that he is, in fact, the man behind this."

"Okay," she said, but she didn't move from his arms, almost as if she was as reluctant to pull away from him as he was to let her go.

"I'll have Zoey work on our side. She can dig around. See what she comes up with." As he spoke, he wasn't really thinking about anything other than how she smelled of fresh sheets and shampoo.

He didn't recall her taking a shower since they had gotten to the house, but at some point, she must have. He took a deep breath, pulling the scent of her soap deep into his lungs.

"You smell good," he said as lust stirred in his body.

Though he was well aware that this wasn't the time, he couldn't help himself. He wanted her. More, he wanted to sweep her up into his arms and carry her away from all the stress filling their lives. He wanted to be her hero. He wanted to be her lover…until the end of time.

Leaning closer as she looked up at him, their eyes met. From the way she gazed at him, he could see that she felt the same confusion, the same needs and the same wants.

He grazed his lips over hers, soft and questioning, making sure that he wasn't misreading her.

She moved into him, reaching up and taking hold of his hair with her hand, pulling his lips hard against hers.

Damn, it felt good.

He leaned back slightly as he thought of everything he had just told her. "I'm sorry, Mindy. About your brother and all the deception."

Her lips moved into a smile as they brushed against his. "Shut up, Jarrod Martin. Just shut up and make love to me."

There was no misreading that.

She must have needed a respite from the confusion as much as he did. And though he questioned whether or not this was a good idea, his body and its desires held precedence over the logical part of his mind—sometimes a man needed to follow his heart.

She pressed him down onto the bed and straddled him. He took hold of her hips as she moved her body over his, reminding him exactly what part of his body was in charge at the moment.

"Mmm," she moaned, rocking back against him.

She was wearing his old Nirvana T-shirt and as she moved, he could make out the subtle curves of her breasts and the hardening of her nipples. Oh, how he wanted to take those little nubs and run them over his lips before popping them in his mouth. He could almost hear her now, moaning his name as he flicked her nipples with his tongue until she was nearly in pain with ecstasy.

She leaned down and he ran his hands up her sides, pulling her lips into his and driving his hips against her so she could feel exactly what it was that she did to him.

Damn, he wanted her.

He kissed her lips and then positioned her head so he could trail his lips down her neck. As he kissed her, her lips found his neck as well and he could feel the subtle graze of her teeth against his skin as though she threatened to devour him. The sensation made him groan with both desire and warning.

"No teeth," he groaned.

"Just like you, Jarrod Martin," she said into the crease of his neck, letting her hot breath brush against his skin where she had just played rough. "I do what I want."

He laughed, and as his body moved, she shifted on him, reminding him exactly who was in control.

He could only love her more for it.

"I hope you realize that I have wanted this, and you, from the first moment I laid eyes on you," he said, pressing himself against the thin fabric of her panties.

"Is that right?" She shifted off him and he reached after her, but she playfully moved out of his reach. "What is it that you want exactly, sir?"

He wasn't sure what game she was playing with him right now, but he liked it. "Well, ma'am, I want to watch you take off your shirt."

"Oh, yeah, is that right?" She reached down and toyed with the edge of the shirt. "How badly?"

"So badly, that if you don't, I may just have to

rip it off you. And that's one of my favorite shirts."
He smiled.

"You would be willing to destroy your favorite
shirt just to get to me?" she teased.

"That's the least of the things that I would do
to make love to you."

"Oh, is that where you think this is leading?"
She lifted the edge of the shirt higher, over her
belly button, exposing a pair of fresh black lace
underwear. They weren't the same kind as before;
rather, they hugged her hips like a pair of hands.
Exactly where his fingers ached to be.

"I believe it was you who told me to make love
to you, ma'am." He grumbled, reaching for her
again, but instead of giving in, she moved farther
from him on the bed.

"If you are lucky, I just may let you. But you are
going to have to play your cards right, *sir.*"

He threw himself back into the pillow, groaning
as he ran his hands over his face and tried to regain
control over the flood of desire he was feeling.

She brushed her fingertips against his legs and
up his thighs. She found the elastic band of his
pajama pants and, running her fingers under it,
pressed the fabric down his legs and over his feet.
He heard the fabric hit the floor beside the bed.

"Do you like it when I play with you?" she
asked.

He uncovered his face and looked up at her. "I

would like it better if you would take off your shirt before I have to do it for you."

She laughed, the sound high and unmarred by the world outside of his bedroom. Humming a little song like something from a risqué movie, she lifted the edges of her shirt until he could see the bottoms of her breasts. Rubbing her hands over her nipples, she gave him an impish smile. "Is this off enough for you?"

He reached for her, and this time she didn't pull away. "Hardly," he said, his voice gravelly and harsh with want.

He kissed the little space between her breasts. The skin was soft. She arched like she was begging for more than his kiss. Running his lips over her skin, he found the curve of her breast as he moved his other hand under her shirt and thumbed her nipple gently as he moved his face back and ran the scruff of his goatee against the little trail of wetness his kiss had left behind.

Her body stiffened at the sensation of soft and scratchy.

"Yes," she whispered.

Not daring to play nice, he took hold of her hips and moved her back on top of him. He pressed himself against her, only a slip of fabric between them.

It didn't escape him that all he had to do to enter her was press the cloth to the side. But no, he had to take this stolen moment for all it was worth. If this was the only time they made love, he wanted to make it the best she'd ever had.

Pushing up her shirt, she took hold of it, and lifted it over her head, exposing her body to the cool midmorning air.

Her nipples were the color of cherry drops. Leaning in, he sucked one into his mouth. It tasted almost as sweet as it looked.

Damn, he was one lucky man.

She shifted against him, but he didn't play along. Instead, he moved his hand down her belly and moved her panties to the side. Ever so gently, he thumbed her as he had thumbed her nipple. Her body was taken with a gentle but sharp spasm as he found and worked her.

"Mmm," she said, her head leaning back as he stroked her. "Yes, Jarrod, yes." Her words were like satin, smooth and silky, giving away the pleasure she must have been feeling beneath his touch.

"I'm yours, my lady. This day, this time, is for your pleasure." He slipped his fingers inside of her as his thumb continue to circle.

She moaned, and the sound made her shudder against his fingers. If he had his way, it wouldn't take long to satisfy her…the first time. And once she found release, he would enter her and hopefully make her find the edge once again.

Gently, and without stopping, he flipped her

over so that she lay open for him. For a brief moment, he paused and stripped her panties from her
so that he could have complete access to her naked
body.

He sat there, gazing at her. He loved the subtle
curves of her waist and that place where they met
the luscious roundness of her hips. She really was
a thing of beauty.

Moving between her legs, his mouth found
where his thumb had been. She tasted even sweeter
than her nipples had. In fact, he could think of nothing more delicious. It was as if they were made for
one another—each the other's nectar and ambrosia.

She moved beneath him, taking his head in her
hands and moving him exactly where and to the
speed she liked.

"Yes, Jarrod, yes…" she moaned quietly.

Just when he thought he couldn't find anything
hotter, she had to go and moan his name like that.

Her breath caught, and he could feel her body
shift and sway under his mouth.

She stiffened as her body pulsed with his touch
as she found the place he had been leading her.

He kissed away her wetness and she pulled him
up to her lips. There was something kinky and
hotter than hell in the way she kissed him, and it
made him love her more. It was a special woman
who wanted to share in everything.

Releasing him from their kiss, he moved down her body and rested his head on her heart. For a moment, he lay there, listening to her heart and the rhythm that told him how he had made her feel. He had done it, brought her to this place of joy and relaxation.

"You can hardly think we're done," she said, her voice swathed in the remnants of euphoria. "One cannot have true pleasure without the other."

He grew impossibly harder at the promise laced in her words.

"That's where we disagree," he teased. "Nothing pleases me more than watching you turn to putty under my touch."

She giggled and he looked up from her chest. "Is that what I am to you?"

He laughed. "And what am I to you?"

She opened her mouth to speak, but he could see a storm cloud roll into her eyes, and she closed her mouth as though she were second-guessing herself.

"Nothing?" he teased, hoping that she would open up to him.

"If I'm putty," she said, her impish smile returning, "then you are the form that I shape myself upon." She sat up, moving atop him. She dipped him slowly into her.

If he had his way, this is how he would be taken from this world…spending the day in bed with the woman he loved and buried deep within her.

No matter what happened in their future, he would be forever thankful that, for now, they were one.

Chapter Seventeen

By the time she was dressed and ready to go downstairs it was approaching evening. The smell of hot food had drifted up from the kitchen and she realized she was starving.

As they made their way into the dining room, Zoey gave them a knowing and highly entertained grin. Anya was sitting in a booster seat beside her and there was a swath of half-colored pages that had been ripped from a coloring book spread around the table.

"You guys have a nice day?" Zoey's smile widened. "I hope you got everything sorted."

Jarrod cleared his throat as a rush of embarrassment burned through Mindy. She hadn't thought about the rest of the household. Really, how could she have when she had been gifted hours in the comfort of Jarrod's embrace?

That man certainly knew his way around her body. If she had another chance, perhaps he could show her again all the ways he could make her feel with just his thumb.

Anya turned toward her. "Anta!" she cried, throwing her hands up in the air and dropping her crayon on the dining room floor.

"Hi, little one, did you have fun with Ms. Zoey today?" she asked, moving over to the girl and giving her a quick hug.

"Uh-huh," Anya said, reaching for Mindy's hand with her pudgy fingers.

They were sticky with what Mindy could only assume was peanut butter and jelly, Anya's favorite afternoon snack.

"Thank you, Zoey, for watching her for me." Mindy let go of Anya's hand and, wiping her hand off on her jeans, sat down across the table from her.

"No problem," Zoey said with a nod. "While you guys were *working* I found some things I thought you all might find interesting."

Mindy tried to ignore the feeling of embarrassment that filled her. Just because Zoey assumed she knew what they were up to upstairs, it didn't mean that there was anything to be ashamed of. She and Jarrod were both adults and they both... Well, they both had to know that there wasn't any possibility of a future. No matter how badly she wanted there to be one.

Though she had forgiven him and they had

made love, there remained a gap between them. Perhaps it was the fact that he had lied to her, or maybe it was something else, but there was something that was making her hold back from falling completely and utterly in love.

"Anta, we see Dada?" Anya said, reaching for another crayon.

And there it was, the wedge that was driving her and Jarrod apart.

There was nothing she could do to bring them together when a child stood in the world between them. Now that she knew Daniel was dead, she had to focus on Anya. She was the only person the little girl had left. First, Anya had been discarded by her mother, and now, with the death of her father, she was completely alone. If something happened to Mindy, she would have no one.

The world had already taken enough from Anya. Mindy couldn't let her be hurt more.

But she also couldn't keep the truth from the little one about her father's death. She had the right to know that her father was gone. Yet, Mindy couldn't bring herself to utter the words that would undoubtedly break Anya's sweet heart.

"I don't think you are going to see him today," Zoey said, seeing Mindy struggle for words.

"Okay," Anya said.

Relief passed through her. Though she should have been honest with Anya, the truth could wait.

There were so many things happening right now, not to mention the fact that Daniel's body hadn't been released to his family. As far as the government was concerned, she had yet to find out about her brother's death.

Sometimes, a reprieve could be found in the shadows of truth.

"You color for a bit, okay?" Zoey said, but Anya barely acknowledged her; instead, she leaned down and started chaotically coloring the picture of a cat. Zoey stood and motioned them to follow her outside.

As they walked out, they noticed a car waiting in the driveway. "Who's that?" Jarrod asked, pointing toward the blue sedan.

"This is your driver," Zoey said, walking them to the car. "He is going to take you to your private jet." She stopped, clearly not planning to elaborate.

"No," Mindy said. "I can't leave Anya."

Zoey sent her an acknowledging smile. "Don't worry about Anya. She and I are going to go over to Dunrovin Ranch. We have family there, including kids that she can play with. We will hole up there until you find Arthur and *neutralize* the situation."

Was she saying that she thought the only solution for Arthur and the spying was to kill him?

Jarrod stopped before they reached the car. "What did you find out about him?"

Zoey glanced over at her brother. "I dug into H&K's records and found—"

"Wait," Mindy said, cutting her off. "How did you gain access to our records?"

Zoey gave a dry laugh. "Did you really think I gave you that phone without a way to keep track of what you did with it?"

So, she had been hacked by the Martins, as well. Mindy sighed. Maybe one day she would no longer be surprised by the family that seemed willing to do anything to get to the answers they needed.

Their family was one that she would have liked to have called her own. Instead, she'd had a globe-trotting brother and a father who had kept them out from underfoot to such an extent that she was only just learning how dangerous his world had been.

"If you could gain access so easily how do we know it was Arthur who stole the data?" Mindy asked.

"Do a lot of people have access to your phone or your personal computer?" Zoey asked, a frown darkening her face.

"No, but—"

"And what about your brother's network? Did anyone have access?" Zoey pressed.

Mindy shook her head. "Daniel didn't have an assistant who had access. Anything that came through his secretary went through separate channels. With Arthur, on the other hand, I thought he could only access certain emails."

"From everything you and my brother have told me, and from what I've been able to piece together, Arthur is our man," Zoey said. "He is definitely up to something at H&K. Now, whether or not that is obtaining and selling military secrets is up for debate, but I have a feeling that we are going to get to the bottom of this soon enough."

Mindy wasn't sure that she had the same level of faith as Zoey, but she also didn't have the same access to data as Jarrod's sister.

Once again, she was thrust into a position where she was being forced to trust this family.

It hadn't even been twenty-four hours since the truth had been supplied to her, and yet there wasn't time to waste rehashing any wrongs. She had granted her forgiveness, but was she ready to trust them?

"Okay," Mindy said, taking a deep breath to alleviate the stress and anxiety that filled her. It did little to help. "But if something happens to me, I want Anya to stay with your family. She doesn't have anyone else. Fake adoption papers, fake whatever you have to, but I don't want her going back to Russia, or falling prey to a broken foster care system. Do I have your word?" Mindy took one more look in through the living room window at the little girl coloring at the dining room table.

"Don't worry. No matter what, I have your daughter under my care. If anyone dares lay a finger on her, I will kill them." Zoey reached up and took hold of Mindy's shoulder. "I will take care of her as if she was my own."

Zoey's words ripped at her. If she'd had the chance, she might have said the same thing to her brother before his death. Instead, he had likely died not knowing what the Fates held in store for the ones he loved.

Once again, she found herself not wishing to follow in her brother's footsteps.

ZOEY HADN'T WHISPERED a single word to him about her plan. No doubt, she had thought it best if he and Mindy didn't know what was in store for them, but it pissed him off. Once again he was reminded of what it must have felt like for Mindy to be kept in the dark.

He and his brothers and sisters, before Trish's death, had prided themselves on not falling into the trap created by keeping secrets. They had all vowed that they would not keep things from one another. Yet, here they were, and here he was once again having to confront his sister's desire to lead the family.

Maybe he shouldn't fight her on it anymore.

Then again, there could only be one leader. More than that would lead to chaos.

Maybe the best thing Jarrod could do was to let Zoey take the controls. She could prove herself, or else she could learn exactly how hard it was to keep order within the family, especially with so much happening right now.

This could be her moment to sink or swim.

If she succeeded, then he could step back and finally enjoy living without the constant pressure of leading the family. He could relax and maybe even follow his heart with Mindy.

For once, he wouldn't have to fight with her. If nothing else, that was a win.

"Before we go anywhere, Zoey," he said, "where are you sending us?"

"With how much we've been through lately, and the liability that comes with running tech, I'm only going to tell you this once, and in person." Zoey glanced toward the car that was waiting for them. "I tracked down Arthur. He's holed up in a hotel room in Stockholm."

"What is he doing there?" Mindy asked.

"From what we know about him," Zoey said, "he's probably getting off US soil in case the CIA chooses to crack down on him for his role in your brother's death."

"But why Sweden?" Jarrod asked.

Zoey shrugged. "Your guess is as good as mine."

He couldn't help but wonder if Arthur was

deeper into this than even he had imagined. What if he had something to do with the hit on Hans Anders, as well?

Maybe he had intended for Mindy and Jarrod to get caught up and killed in the melee.

On some level it made sense. It seemed more than possible that after killing Daniel, Arthur had decided to go after Jarrod, as well. At Camp Delta, the day Daniel had died, there hadn't been cameras rolling. Which meant that Jarrod was the only witness to Daniel's murder.

That, in and of itself, was more than enough motive for Arthur to want him dead.

He couldn't wait to get on the plane, fly across the Atlantic and lay a beatdown on the man.

He took Mindy's hand and led her toward the sedan that was waiting. "We will be back here as soon as we can," he said to Zoey as she walked the last few feet to the car with him. "While I'm gone, you are running things. She and I will be off devices as much as we can to keep anyone from tracking us."

"Just call me when you can. You are going to have a stop in New York before heading over the Atlantic, but from what the pilot has said, it sounds like you'll be there by tomorrow morning, their time."

"Do you have any clue how to find Arthur when

we get there?" Mindy asked, opening the car door and putting one leg inside.

"According to the app OpenTable, he made a reservation for tomorrow night at the Wine Cellar at the Grand Hôtel," Zoey said, helping her into the car. "You both have bags packed and waiting for you on the plane. If you need anything, use cash. Stay off the radar as much as possible." She closed the door on Mindy's side of the car.

"Thank you," Jarrod said, realizing how much work his sister must have done. "Seriously, I appreciate it."

"No matter what happens, you will always be my big brother, Jarrod." She threw her arms around him and gave him a hug.

From the way she held on to him, he could sense that she was frightened. With all their ups and downs, he hadn't really realized how much Zoey loved him.

"I love you, sis. Take care of things while we're gone." He gave her a quick kiss on the cheek.

"You got it." Zoey let go of him and watched as he got into the car. "And hey, bro, make sure you and Mindy come back safe. I want to watch you two get married."

Chapter Eighteen

The flight felt short, but it could have been because he and Mindy had spent most of it locked in the back bedroom making love until they had both fallen fast asleep.

The pilot had made a stop to refuel at a private airstrip near NYC, but he and the staff aboard the plane had done little to interfere with their private time.

Jarrod couldn't have thanked them enough, and when the pilot announced their descent into Stockholm, a profound sadness filled him.

He glanced over at Mindy. Her green eyes were heavy with sleep. She gave him a drowsy and satisfied smile. "Good morning," she said, "are you ready for this?"

All he was ready for was to live his entire life with her in his arms. Screw the world and all the madness within it.

He knew that was impossible. They had to go

back to their lives. And that meant he had to make sure Arthur was no longer a danger to Mindy—and that meant that he had to clear her name of any possible wrongdoing.

His family's plan was to come together at the Widow Maker Ranch and live out their days in seclusion and peace. At least until the Gray Wolves were under control and they were no longer in fear for their lives. As such, once everything was handled with Arthur and Mindy was once again safe, she could come back to the ranch. If she was willing. He knew she had an entire business to run on her own, thanks to Daniel's death.

Their time together might be coming to a close. Sure, they could try the long-distance thing, but such relationships were often destined to fail. Life always got in the way. First, they would go out of their way to meet up together—missing meetings and throwing caution to the wind. But over time, when the bloom left the rose, business would once again come first and life would take over. They would slowly move apart until neither could really recall exactly why they had ever gotten together in the first place.

It was better to realize now that whatever they had would be best left behind. It would be easier on both of them, instead of deluding themselves into thinking that they could make it work—no matter how much he loved her.

She blinked, her impossibly long eyelashes brushing against her cheeks. He wished he could tell her how he felt, that he loved her, that he wanted to be hers forever, and that he would do anything for her.

However, if he gave in now and told her how he was really feeling, it wouldn't just be him that he was hurting…and he had promised that he would do anything to stop her from being hurt further. He had to keep his word.

The plane jerked as the wheels touched down on the tarmac.

Mindy set about getting her clothes together and putting them on as he watched. If things went well, they might very well be bringing Arthur back with them on their next plane ride. This could be their last time alone.

Reaching over, he helped her button her pants. And before she could turn away, he took her one more time into his arms and gave her a kiss that felt entirely too much like goodbye. She looked up at him as he let her go. There were questions in her eyes, and behind those questions was a darkness as she, too, must have realized what he had been thinking.

She knew as well as he did that what they had together was over.

The ride to their hotel was quiet and filled with melancholy. They passed by beautiful waterside and antiquated architecture, which would have normally given him joy. This time all he could think about was the sadness that filled him.

Maybe he could move to New York and stay with her and Anya. But then, she hadn't spoken of a future together. And just like him, she was probably guarding herself from becoming too emotionally attached. That, or she held no feelings for him at all.

It pained him to realize the truth of their arrangement.

He normally wasn't the kind of man who fell for a woman, so maybe this was his karma. In a way, he couldn't deny that he deserved what he was getting from her.

Though she had seemed to forgive him for his transgressions, she had never really told him so in as many words.

Maybe she had spent the night with him to ensure that he would be hurt as badly as she was. Or perhaps she had taken him in an attempt to make herself feel better and to forget about the pain in her real life. Maybe she had known it was over before it began.

As their car came to a stop in front of the hotel, he looked across the water to the royal palace. It was no coincidence that Arthur was here. He had to have been somehow involved with the Riksdag, or possibly Hans Anders's murder.

Come hell or high water, Jarrod would get to the bottom of this.

Not for the first time, he wished he could call his people at the CIA. He wished there was somebody he could trust to be on his side and tell him more about Arthur.

If Arthur really was a double agent, then it seemed likely he may have also been behind the suspicion of Daniel and Mindy. Perhaps Arthur had even been spreading rumors that she was somehow involved with Hans's murder, and in an effort to expunge himself from any possible guilt, he was here trying to sell his innocence to this Swedish Parliament.

Bottom line, Arthur was a bastard.

In broken Swedish, he thanked his driver and helped Mindy out of the car. The driver motioned that he would be taking the bags into the hotel for them. Jarrod handed him a healthy tip in kronor.

The man took the money with a wide smile and stuffed it into his pocket before escorting them to the lobby door where a bellman waited. The driver said something to the man and, though the well-dressed bellman was already at attention, he stood a bit straighter.

"If you wouldn't mind," Jarrod said, "could you please make sure our bags arrive safely in our rooms?" He handed the bellman the same tip he had given the driver.

The bellman nodded, and the money disappeared as though in the hands of a well-practiced magician.

They weren't at a HoJo in the States, that was for sure.

As they made their way into the foyer, they were met with brilliant marble floors, fresh-cut flowers and crystal chandeliers that cascaded down from the ceilings. The place was quiet, though a few guests were making their way to and from the elevators and up and down the grand staircase. The hotel smelled of something clean but dripping of class, something reminiscent of white tea and sage. The palatial foyer opened up into a group of rooms and the luxury hotel's front desk, where a woman in a suit waited with a smile.

He would have to ensure that he had the right attire for such a place. The thought made him miss the ranch, and it reminded him of just another thing that was so different from NYC and Mindy's life. With her lace panties and high-end clothes—well, all except his Nirvana shirt—she was totally out of place at a Montana ranch.

He slipped his hand into hers, pretending just for a moment that they were something more than what they could be.

She gave his hand a squeeze as she smiled over at him, and, though they were both terribly underdressed, he found himself right at home. He had her.

When they checked into their rooms, they were booked as Mr. and Mrs. Martino. He couldn't help but notice the faint rosiness rise in her cheeks at the moniker that his sister had assigned them.

Maybe it wasn't so crazy to hope that she had feelings for him that went beyond a one-night stand.

Taking their respective keys, they made their way up to the suite Zoey had reserved for them. The main room was enormous, and it looked out upon the waterway and the palace. He hated to think how much this would be costing the company. If he had been alone, he would have not put himself up in such a magnificent room. But he was glad his sister had chosen this for them. If nothing else, he and Mindy could spend their last night together in the lap of luxury. Perhaps she would think that he wasn't that different from her after all.

The door clicked shut behind them and as it did, he could hear the air rush from Mindy. "Wow," she whispered.

"Zoey did well." He chuckled. "I think she'll manage to take care of everything while I'm gone."

"Is that her role in your family, to make sure everything runs smoothly?" Mindy asked, walking across the large room and stopping in front of the window. "I would have assumed you were the head of the family."

Did she just implicitly know where his sore spots were, or had he let something slip during their time together?

"I'm oldest, but as you can see I'm hardly the one in control."

"Actually, I know a little bit about that, as well." She moved the leather chair that sat beside the window and motioned for him to come sit beside her.

"Oh, really? But you work under your brother. I thought—"

"He was my boss? Yes, he definitely was. He ran the company. But in our personal lives, he was always a bit of a mess. I mean, look at Anya, for example." She turned to him as he sat down beside her. "I've always had to step up when it comes to him. It was the main reason that I never really wanted to be a part of my father's company."

Every time he thought he knew this woman, she surprised him, and that enigmatic quality was just one of the many reasons that losing her would tear his guts out.

If there was even a chance that he could make a future with her, he would seize it with both hands. And no matter what happened, he would fight.

Chapter Nineteen

They arrived early to the dining room and, after giving the hostess what Mindy knew to be at least a thousand dollars in kronor, they made their way to a private table. From where they sat, they had a perfect view of the wine cellar and yet were out of sight from anyone who sat below.

Thankfully, when she had unpacked the bag Zoey must have curated, she had found a red Chanel dress, complete with matching heels and a clutch. She couldn't have picked a more dazzling or sexy dress herself. As she sat down, the hem of the dress threatened to expose more of her backside than she desired. In an attempt at modesty, she perched forward on her seat until the hostess had retired from their room.

Jarrod, having noticing her predicament, made his way around the table and helped her stand. She adjusted her dress slightly and found her proper seat. "Thank you, my kind sir," she said with a forced formal air.

"You know what happens when you start calling me sir," he teased, giving her a mischievous grin. "This may be a private dining room, but I doubt that's what they have in mind." He touched her bare shoulder and his warm fingers made her cool skin prickle to life. "But, hey, if you're game, you know I am."

She laughed, the sound bouncing around the walls of the small stone room, making it sound more like the morose cascade of raindrops.

As though he, too, heard the faint sadness in the sound, he stopped smiling and sat down. "But really," he said, looking around the centerpiece, "you look beautiful."

She ran her hands down the satin of her dress, straightening some invisible wrinkle. "Thank you. Your sister has good taste."

"I like you in that dress almost as much as I'd like you out of it," he said, giving her the same look he had when he'd first kissed her lips.

If she could have caught that look in a memory and saved it in her soul, she would have. But, as it was…

"Jarrod, are you going to be okay?" she asked. She wanted to reach across the table and take his hand, which wouldn't be smart, knowing what she needed to say.

"What do you mean? Because I'm imagining you out of that dress?" He grinned, but she could see in his eyes that he knew exactly where this conversation was going. "You may give me a heart attack, but I think I'll recover."

She couldn't help the little smile that played on her lips. "No, you know what I mean."

He sighed, unfolding the linen napkin that was in the shape of a swan and placing it in his lap. Though she was certain that it was some nervous tic and a way for him to evade the topic, she followed suit.

"Jarrod, when we get home…"

"I know. I know," he said, resignation in his tone. "I've not been able to think of anything else since we landed. I've worked this through a million different ways."

"But you know how this has to end, just as much as I do—don't you?" she asked.

He nodded. "But do we really have to talk about it?"

He was right. There was no sense hashing over their destiny. Some battles were lost before a person could ever even step foot on the battlefield.

Still, what she truly wanted was for him to tell her that she was wrong. That they could make this work. That if they both just believed in love enough, they could triumph over whatever obstacles stood in their way. She wanted him to tell her that love—their love—was all it would take for both of them to find true happiness and peace.

Even though their lives had been in upheaval since they had met, she couldn't deny that what they had was special. Jarrod knew it, as well. That was what was making this just that much harder.

She had been waiting all of her life to meet a man like him, a man who could make her laugh at the lowest points in her life, a man who could make her forgive even the greatest missteps with the simple curve of his smile. She hadn't truly believed in soul mates…that was, until she had met him. Now she couldn't imagine her life or her future without him. He had become as much a part of her as her soul. If the world was to strip him away from her, she would be left with an empty shell.

She needed him to be whole.

But she couldn't argue with what had to be. There was no sense in pursuing something that was fated to die.

She'd had her fair share of relationships in the past. Long-distance didn't work. Relocating would be difficult for either of them, and unless he felt as strongly about her as she did him, it would be pointless. He couldn't. If he did, how could he be sitting there ever so calmly and staring at her with those big blue eyes?

She had to let him go. For the sake of her own heart, there was no other choice. If she didn't keep the last little bits of her guard up, she would end up as battered as the stone walls that surrounded them. No matter how hard she tried to grasp at the sounds of laughter, everything would turn into the sandy rasp of a mournful wail.

Their sommelier came up and, in heavily accented English, gave them the list of wines that the cellar was serving that night. The bottles ranged in price from moderate to so expensive that they hadn't bothered to put the prices on the list—including a Bordeaux from 1794.

She ordered the chardonnay and he followed suit. As the waiter disappeared, Jarrod turned back to her. From the look on his face he wanted to say something, no doubt wanting to continue their conversation from before. She couldn't bring herself to give it any more energy.

"What are we going to do with Arthur?" As she changed the subject, Jarrod's features drooped.

"On the slim chance that he actually shows up… To be honest, I haven't got a clue." He peered over the ledge of the private balcony and to the cellar below. "I have to admit, I haven't been giving this enough headspace. I think my mind has been on other, more pressing, matters."

As was hers. If she had her way, Arthur wouldn't show. At least not now. Instead, they could spend one more night together.

"This place totally reminds me of one of those

episodes on *The Bachelor* where the man takes
the woman on a one-on-one," she said, motioning
around the romantic cellar and the racks of wine
that adorned its walls. "Think about it. We could
do the whole thing…a band, fireworks at the end
of the night…" *And a one-way ticket to the fantasy suite.*

"Don't tell me you're into reality television," he
said with a soft laugh.

"Hey now," she teased, "we are all allowed one
vice. Mine just happens to be that I love to watch
modern-day romances, no matter how screwed up
the premise. I mean what woman would patiently
wait for a man to take her on a date while he's busy
bedding other women?"

He laughed.

"But," she continued, "if you ignore all that
nonsense, it really is a cute love story." She took
a sip of the water that was sitting on the table as
they waited for their wine. "Can you imagine telling
your children that you spent your dates in foreign
countries, at private concerts by big-name talent,
and falling in love?"

"Except for the big-name talent and fireworks
bit, I think that you and I would be able to tell our
children exactly that," he said.

She felt the air rush from her lungs as the sommelier brought out the chardonnay that they had
requested and poured them each a taste.

Had Jarrod really just insinuated that he was falling in love with her, that *they* could have children together? Her chest tightened with giddiness.

She sniffed the wine as the sommelier waited for the approval on their wine selection, but given the attention she was paying to the wine, she could have been sniffing turpentine.

"Will this selection work for you?" the sommelier asked, holding the bottle at arm's length in front of her so she could see the label.

She nodded, afraid that if she actually tried to speak her words would come out as a high-pitched, excited squeak.

The waiter appeared from around the corner and entered their room as the sommelier left the bottle and made his way from the table. "Sir, madam, it is my pleasure to serve you this evening." As the man gave them the preamble of specials and what kind of cuts of meat they were serving in the restaurant that evening, she inched her toes out of her shoe and moved it under the table to find Jarrod's foot. She ran her stockinged toes under the edge of his suit pants and up his leg.

He gave her a look of lusty surprise just as the waiter stopped talking. The waiter stood waiting for him to speak, but Jarrod appeared panicked, as though he had been paying as little attention to the man as she had.

"Um, yes, thank you." Jarrod waved away the

menu the man offered. "Instead of picking, would you please have the chef prepare whatever dish he recommends for us this evening?"

Apparently, Jarrod liked to live dangerously even when it came to gastronomies. She wouldn't be surprised if the dinner came out and was comprised of sweetbreads and other mystery meats. But what did it matter? As it was, she wasn't feeling hungry for anything other than the look he kept giving her as she ran her foot farther up his leg.

Even though the waiter couldn't possibly have seen what was happening under the table, he promptly took his leave. She couldn't have been more grateful.

There were the sounds of men's voices as someone entered the main cellar area below. Peeking over the edge, the bald head of a man came into view. As the man turned, she could make out his round, pudgy features. She recognized him as one of the members of the Swedish parliament from the meeting that they had held in the city. Though she couldn't remember the man's name, she recalled that he was one of Hans's subordinates and the next in line to the man's seat.

Walking behind the man, she recognized her former assistant, Arthur McDuffy—if that was his real name. "Look," she whispered.

The sight of him made bile rise up in her throat, and she forced herself to sit back, hiding herself from the men below. From the smattering of voices, they were part of a larger group.

Chairs scraped on the stone floor as the men sat down. She could hear Arthur making small talk with the men around him. They spoke of the weather, their flights and the state of their families. It drove her mad.

She moved to stand, to charge downstairs and face the man head-on. What did it matter? They didn't have a plan. Instead, Jarrod reached out and took her by the hand, stopping her. He shook his head.

She considered shoving his hand aside, but she stopped. She couldn't think about just herself—she had to think about Jarrod and his safety, as well. And that was to say nothing of Anya, who waited at home for them. She promised herself that she wouldn't leave the girl alone. That meant that she would have to handle this situation with caution.

No matter how badly she wanted to go in with guns blazing.

It felt like justice—to kill the man who had killed her brother.

If she was lucky, she would still get the chance. However, if she attacked right now she was more likely to go to prison than she was to get her revenge.

She had to play this smart. Jarrod motioned for her to come near him so he could whisper in her ear.

"When Arthur attacked your brother and killed him, your brother was reaching for this." Jarrod reached into his pocket and extracted a pen and a photo of her.

She swayed on her impossibly high heels. Jarrod took her by the waist and made her sit on his knee. He wrapped his arm around her. "You're going to be okay," he whispered.

"But why? Why did he have this?" She paused. "And where did you get it?"

"Zoey can get her hands on almost anything. Seriously." He chuckled. She had no doubt that Zoey was capable of anything. The woman was a powerhouse.

"Do you recognize the pen?" he asked as she took her picture from Jarrod's hand. There was a splatter of blood on the bottom, just over her heart. She tried to not think of it as a sign, but rather as her brother's attempt to remind her of exactly what she had to lose.

She glanced over at the pen still in Jarrod's hand. It was silver and rather unremarkable. She shook her head. "I don't think so. Why?"

He let go of her and twisted the pen open. Instead of a regular nib at the end, the pen had a white capsule at its tip. He closed the pen's nib, like he somehow feared its contents.

"What is it? The powder, I mean?" she asked, motioning toward the pen, fearful of touching it.

"At the time, I didn't know. I assumed it was some sort of cyanide capsule."

She stared at her reflection in the pen's mirrored surface. "Do you think he was trying to kill himself? To die instead of allow you to interrogate him?"

"I don't know if he was intending on using it on himself or on Arthur, but before he had the chance, Arthur shot him."

She covered her mouth with her hands as she tried to work through everything Jarrod was telling her. "Why didn't you tell me all this before?"

He put the pen back into his pocket. "I didn't think it mattered. Until now I thought it was just one of those details that didn't play into the larger picture. That was until I found out about Arthur."

"And now?" she asked between the spaces in her fingers.

"Well, with the attack on Hans," he said, motioning toward the men who were still talking loudly below, "I'm wondering if the powder inside this pen might be linked to the nerve agent attack."

"Do you think Arthur planted it on my brother? That he intended on poisoning him? Then us?"

"I thought about that," Jarrod said, nodding. "In some ways it makes sense. Maybe Arthur had hoped to kill him with it. Or maybe Daniel had it before he stepped into the interrogation room. And

I can't help wondering if your picture is somehow tied in, as well."

He turned the photo over, revealing the threatening note.

It appeared that her brother had died trying to protect her.

She started to stand, but he stopped her. "I didn't tell you this so you would fly off the rails. Right now, I need you to stay on point with me. Don't let your emotions get us into trouble."

She reminded herself of the Swedish prison that waited for her if something went wrong downstairs. "Okay," she said, trying to quell her rage. "What is it that you think we should do?"

"We need to get Arthur alone."

"I've got it." She stood up, this time resolved to keep herself from flying off into a murderous rage…at least for now.

If they did this right, they could take Arthur down. She would have to be patient. In fact, they could probably kill him and be out of the country before anyone was any the wiser.

Their waiter returned carrying a tray of bacon-wrapped figs covered in warm honey. He set them down on the table between them. "Compliments of the chef. And he wishes you the most wonderful of evenings. He is looking forward to enrapturing your senses with tonight's delicacies."

Mindy forced a polite smile. "Please extend him our gratitude."

As the waiter turned, Jarrod called to him. "Excuse me?"

"Yes, sir," the waiter said, turning back to face them.

"Would you please tell the man, the one in the dark suit in the lower room, that she—" he motioned to Mindy "—wishes to meet him in the hall?"

The waiter glanced over at her and gave her a presuming smile. "Absolutely."

"Along with her invitation, would you please include a glass of one of your finest wines?"

"Sir, our wines are sold by the bottle."

"Then, by all means, please present him with the bottle."

The waiter gave a well-practiced bow. "And may I ask who is sending the bottle, sir?"

She moved closer to the waiter. "Just tell him it is from his secret admirer."

Admirer or adversary, what was the difference? Right now, all that mattered was taking him down.

The waiter nodded and excused himself from their room.

"You do realize that is likely a hundred-thousand-dollar bottle of wine you just ordered," she said.

"If it gets him out of that room and away from

the other members of the Swedish parliament then I will have to consider it a smart business expense." He smiled. "That's what tax write-offs are for—isn't it?"

"I doubt it will be the first homicide that ended in a tax write-off." She laughed. "I really do need to start taking notes from your playbook." She ran her hands down the front of his suit jacket, and ever so carefully she pulled the pen from his pocket.

He didn't notice as she wrapped it in her hand and held it out of sight.

"I'm at your mercy," he said, with a slight tip of his head.

She didn't question it. For as much as he was at her mercy, she found herself happily following the requests of the man. In a world full of lies and betrayal, they had found each other.

He stood up and took her by the hand. "I'll step into the kitchen while you wait for him in the hall. He may panic when he sees you." He paused to look her straight in the eye. "If you feel in danger in any way I want you to get the hell out of there. You run. Don't try to face him down, and don't do anything stupid, just get him to stay there. If he is the man we think he is, he may come in hot at you."

Though she heard what he was saying and she wanted to heed his warnings, she wasn't sure she would actually be able to do as he asked. "I'll try. You just stay close."

He looked nervous, but maybe that was how she looked, too.

She walked out of their dining area and followed Jarrod to the kitchen door, where he stepped inside. Through the window she could see the kitchen staff had stopped and were staring at Jarrod. With the placement of a bill in the head chef's hand and what she assumed was a thank-you for the figs or possibly a quick explanation of what he was doing in their private sanctum, the staff returned to their normal business hurrying around the kitchen.

That man knew how to grease a palm.

In their high-stakes world, she would do well to learn from him. Maybe one day she would be just as smooth, but for now she had only started.

As she made her way back toward the main cellar, she tried to stay in view of the small circular window that looked out at the hall and to the dining room. Jarrod would have to be careful to remain unseen.

Their waiter made his way out of the main dining room. "He is on his way, madam. Is there anything else you might need from me for now?"

She shook her head. "Thank you."

The waiter returned to the kitchen and disappeared through the door to where Jarrod was waiting.

She stood in the hall for what felt like an hour but was likely only a matter of seconds. Time lost all meaning as she stood there, thinking about Daniel, about the attacks, about Anya and the world she would have to go home to, and all the damage Arthur had done in her life.

Finally Arthur made his way out of the dining room. He was carrying a glass of red wine and as he looked up and saw her, she could have sworn she saw a little ripple in the liquid, as though his hands were starting to shake.

He would have been stupid not to be afraid.

"Ms. Kohl, I didn't know you were going to be here in Stockholm. I thought you were still in the States."

"Ah, no," she said, the mirth dripping from her voice. "Surprise trip. I had to come in and check on the H&K assets. Always doing business…isn't that right, Arthur?"

He moved closer to her but was careful to stay just outside her reach, almost as if he feared she might lash out at him. "When did you arrive in Sweden?" He swallowed hard, making his Adam's apple jump like a bullfrog.

"We just arrived this morning." She gripped the pen in the palm of her hand, swirling it with her fingers and making sure the nib was exposed. If the contents of the pen were cyanide, Arthur would be down and dead within a matter of seconds…probably less than the time it had taken for her brother to die from Arthur's bullet.

"We?" he asked, looking around them.

"I came with a friend, someone who has been looking out for my best interests ever since that horrific event in the city."

Arthur couldn't meet her eye. "Yes, I'm sorry I didn't get to come see you in the hospital. I had—"

"You can hold your excuses and your lies, Agent Arthur. I know exactly who you are and what you've done to my family and my business." She lowered the pen in her fingers, but before she killed him, she had to get her closure. "You've been exposed."

"Is that why you've come here? Because you think I did something to you?" He looked confused, but his gaze darted around the empty hallway. "What have I been exposed as?" he asked, sounding glib.

She couldn't believe that he was trying to act innocent. Ignorance wasn't a defense.

"I found out about your role in Daniel's death."

His mouth dropped open. "I don't know what you are talking about," he said, but now some of the glibness had disappeared from his voice.

He turned his back to the kitchen and she saw Jarrod glance out at them. She gave him an almost imperceptible nod, and at the signal he silently opened the door to the kitchen and moved in behind the man. From under his jacket, he reached behind him and pulled out a handgun. Her time with Arthur was quickly running out.

"I know you killed him. Don't deny that you pulled the trigger. You knew your lies were catching up with you. Danny must have found out about your role in selling our family's secrets to our enemies. I bet that when he figured it out, you had him arrested. I know about your role in the CIA... and that you're working both governments. In fact, I bet you're making a hell of a lot of money." All the weight lifted from her chest, but her hatred for the man remained.

"Mindy, you have me all wrong," he pleaded, putting his free hand up in surrender, like somehow the simple action could save him from her rage.

"I allowed you into my life. You took my secrets... my family's secrets...and you sold them to the highest bidders. Then you murdered my brother in cold blood...and then you tried to kill me with the nerve agent. That was the real reason you suddenly left my side for an 'urgent business trip.' Were you going to North Korea so you could pick up your money?" She gripped the pen in her hand so hard that she could feel the metal clip on its side cutting into her palm.

"If you think that's true, then it's time you get a new source." Arthur leaned around her as if checking to make sure none of the members of parliament were in sight.

"What I can't figure out is why you are here. What business could you have with the Riksdag?"

She tried not to look as Jarrod took another step closer. He raised his gun, aiming it straight for the back of Arthur's head as he waited for her signal.

But she wasn't ready. No. Nor would she be. This was one killer that she had to take down herself. She had to avenge her brother's death.

"I know you think you know everything about me. But trust me when I tell you that you have this all wrong. I'm not the man you think I am."

"Don't you dare ask me to trust you," she seethed.

"You're right, that was the wrong choice of words. But at least hear me out."

As badly as she wanted to jab the pen into his jugular and end him, she found herself wanting to hear. A strange gnawing in her gut told her something wasn't quite right.

"I do work for the CIA. I did kill your brother." He gave her a pleading look and the wine in his glass sloshed against the sides. "I'm sorry. I didn't want to kill your brother. It wasn't my intention."

"But it was the only way you could keep the truth of your corruption from coming to light…"

"No," Arthur argued. "I wasn't the one selling your family's secrets to North Korea. It was Daniel. And you weren't ever supposed to be here."

"Liar." She took a half step toward him.

"No, I have proof. He wasn't acting alone," Arthur said. "Don't do anything stupid. I'm here to—"

He was interrupted by the rattle of rifles and body armor as eight men charged down the hallway and turned into view at the corner by the kitchen. Jarrod turned to them, a look of surprise on his face as he lowered his weapon.

She was shocked. How had she and Jarrod gotten this so wrong? Arthur moved around her and she stepped closer to Jarrod.

"What in the hell is going on?" she whispered, watching as Arthur's team moved in file down the hallway, clearing the doorways as they moved toward the cellar's main dining area.

Arthur turned to Jarrod and nodded. "I should have known that you would get yourself wrapped up in this."

"What are you talking about, Arthur?" Jarrod snarled. "What's going on?"

He turned to face them both. "Mindy, we discovered that your father had been selling secrets for the last five years. When he tried to remove himself from the arrangement with North Korea, they poisoned him. Much like they had planned on poisoning you."

She felt the fight dissolve from her. "You were trying to protect me? If that's true, why did you kill Daniel?"

"Daniel was an unfortunate loss. We hadn't

intended on killing him, but the Koreans were breathing down his neck. We think he went for the pen knowing I would be forced to act and pull the trigger."

"You didn't have to kill him."

"If I hadn't, the Koreans would have… And they probably would have killed you, too."

"And what about the nerve agent attack? I suppose you are going to say that was the Koreans' doing, as well?" Jarrod asked.

"The attack is actually what brought us here." Arthur nodded toward his team. "Your father's and brother's roles in supplying weapons to North Korea had come to light within the Riksdag. That was one of the reasons Hans was going to do everything in his power to shut your company down—and never allow you access to Sweden. Your brother had an agreement with North Korea, and thanks to this the North Koreans stepped in. They needed you to continue your work without any hindrances. They bought several of the members of the parliament and they were the ones who helped arrange the hit. Your brother and his cronies had one hell of a business going—they were making money from every angle." Arthur paused as he gave a stiff, ruthless laugh. "If you think about it, North Korea is part of the reason your family's company is so profitable."

She felt a wave of sickness overtake her as she

realized her entire life had been bought and paid for with blood money.

"Now, I'm here working with the Säkerhetspolisen, or SAPO, and luring out those that the North Koreans had paid to help with the hit," Arthur said, putting his finger to his lips as he handed her his glass of wine. "Stay back. I don't want either of you to get hurt."

Chapter Twenty

There was screwing up and then there was royally screwing things up, and this time he had definitely hit an all-time low. Jarrod holstered his gun as he pulled Mindy close to him. If there was going to be a firefight between the joint task force and the rogue members of the Swedish parliament, he needed to get Mindy out of there.

But as he nudged her to move back toward the kitchen and away from the fight, she refused to budge.

"Jarrod, is Arthur telling the truth? Were my brother and father really doing all that?" she asked, sounding broken.

He stared down the hallway at the joint task force. From what he could see, it looked as though the man at the front of the formation was definitely CIA, as was the man behind him. The next two appeared to be in a different kind of tactical gear, and their weaponry was definitely from UN. Behind them were members of the SAPO.

"From the looks of it, our investigation was only the tip of a much bigger iceberg." He looked at Arthur. "He was right."

"But I thought you said that the CIA sent you to investigate me? How did you not know about the rest of the operation?"

The blood drained from his face. The CIA had used him as their pawn and he had been too stupid to see their game for what it really was. And now he had to admit that he once again wasn't the man she thought he was.

"I think they sent me to keep an eye on you. If they'd really been suspicious, you would have had CIA agents assigned to you. They must have wanted me to keep you out of danger during their raid on your family."

"But...why?"

He sighed. "Like I told you, I'm a government contractor. STEALTH works for groups all over the world just like the CIA. And, as contractors, sometimes our job isn't to know everything that is going on with a case. That's why they call us in, to handle the odds and ends bits that could land them in hot water if they ever fell under investigation. As a contractor, we are held to different standards—especially when working internationally. We don't have to play by the rules of the Geneva Conventions."

"You make it sound like you are badasses."

"And yet, here I stand in front of you looking like a chump." He hung his head playfully before giving her his most melting smile.

"But what about the man in the city? The man in Anya's music class? Was he a part of this, too?"

And the next hatchet fell. *Crap.* He had almost forgotten about the man and the life that was waiting for him when he got back home. "Mindy, you aren't the only one with enemies. I think that man… Actually, I know that man was a member of a group called the Gray Wolves—a group that is actively targeting my family."

"What?" She leaned back against the wall behind them.

From down the hall, Arthur called out to his men and they rushed the dining room, guns aimed at the men inside. There were the sounds of bodies being dropped down to the floor and handcuffs being clicked.

Thankfully, and almost surprisingly, there wasn't the sound of a single round being fired.

Maybe the CIA didn't want to pick up the tab for a rack of hundred-thousand-dollar bottles of wine.

Arthur's mission appeared to be a complete success. Especially compared to STEALTH's handling of the mess.

Though perhaps he was looking at their situation from the wrong angle. Instead of thinking of it as being played by the CIA, he had gotten a once-in-a-lifetime opportunity to spend time with a woman who might be his soul mate.

"Who are the Gray Wolves?" she asked.

"When we were in Turkey on a mission for the CIA, we had a run-in with the Gray Wolves, a Turkish crime syndicate. My sister Trish was killed," he said, emotion clogging his throat. "Well, we managed to take out a lot of their men… and cost the leader and his organization millions of dollars. As a result, they put out a hit on us."

She nodded. "So the man in my apartment and the one from the music class—Gray Wolves? How can you be sure Zoey and Anya are safe?"

"The Gray Wolves don't know about the Montana ranch. We're very careful to keep it that way." He gave her a feeble and apologetic smile. "I'm so sorry, Mindy. I'm sorry that I have made your life such a disaster."

"You *did* do that." She took a long drink from the wineglass Arthur had handed her. She laughed as she caught Jarrod gawking at her. "Did you seriously think that I would let this good a wine go to waste? You really don't know me."

He laughed, thankful that she seemed to finally

find some peace with the situation. If nothing else, perhaps they could be friends when they got back to the States.

She leaned in closer to him and he could smell the rich hues of strawberry and oak from the wine on her breath. "Another thing you may not know about me… I have a thing for men who are real."

"You mean you like *chumps*?" he asked, looking deep into her green eyes.

"Not chumps," she said with a little giggle. "But I've dated enough men who think they are the world's greatest catch…men with more money than they even know what to do with…men who have no real drive in life. I love a man who can take his lumps and admit when he is wrong."

"You mean you could love a man who would take you on a worldwide adventure, only to learn that he had screwed up from the very beginning?"

She leaned even closer to him, her lips on the cusp of his ear. "But wasn't it one hell of an adventure?"

He couldn't deny that fact. Looking back at his career, he'd never missed the mark on a case so badly before. However, this was probably the best case he had ever worked on.

She drew his earlobe into her mouth, giving it a light nibble as she kissed him. "And as far as loving you," she said, letting go of his earlobe. "If you give me half a chance, I could love you until the end of time."

A wide smile took over his face and he wrapped his arms around her, careful not to spill her glass of wine. "Why, Ms. Kohl, I think you're declaring your love for me."

"I know you warned against me calling you sir, and now I see why. If you call me miss one more time I'm going to have to take you upstairs and show you exactly how unladylike I can be."

"Would you rather I call you Mrs.?"

Mindy smiled as she drew back slightly and looked up at him. "Will you marry me?"

"I don't have a ring, and unlike *The Bachelor* I can't give you the final rose. Well, I would, if I had one..." He stammered. Dammit, this was going all wrong. "What I mean is, yeah, I'd love to marry the hell out of you."

She laughed, the sound mixing with the footsteps of the task forces and their detainees as they marched down the hall beside them.

As they walked by, Arthur gave them a wink. "I'll see you guys back in the States. If you need anything, or have any questions, you know where to find me."

Jarrod flipped the guy the bird as he laughed.

All he cared about now was Mindy. "Ms. Kohl, it appears as though we finally may have a bit of time alone."

"And for the moment, it appears no one is trying to murder us."

He laughed. "Are you going to be bored if no one throws nerve agents at us?"

She shook her head, a playful smile on her lips. "Is this what it's going to be like, married to you?"

He couldn't believe this was really happening, that in just a matter of moments his entire life had changed for the better. Even so, he couldn't completely give in to the happiness.

"Are you sure that I'm what you want in your life? I mean, what about Anya?"

She gave him a kiss on the cheek. "I know that you and your family are among the safest places that we could possibly be. But I'm going to need her approval. Oh, and she has to have a spot in our wedding."

"But aren't you going back to NYC? You have the company to worry about…and now that you're down an assistant…"

"I have a feeling that we're going to start moving in a new direction. But I'm not going to worry about any of that right now. Just like the rest of our lives—you and I are going to have to just figure this thing out as we go." She ran her hand down his cheek as their gazes met. "Now, sir, take me upstairs and show me what adventure means to you."

Epilogue

Anya ran out of the front door of the Widow Maker Ranch's main house as they drove up and parked in the driveway. Zoey was close at her heels.

"Anta!" Anya called, throwing her little round hands up into the air as she waited for Mindy to come sweep her into her arms.

"Hi, sweetheart," Mindy called, waving at her niece as she and Jarrod stepped out of the car. "How did it go?" she asked Zoey as she made her way over to Anya and pulled her into her embrace.

The little one smelled of Cheerios and fresh air, and it reminded her of exactly what she wanted for the girl.

"Everything went great. And from the sounds of it, far better than your trip." Zoey gave Jarrod a hug.

Jarrod let go of his sister and sent Mindy a sly grin.

She was glad that they had waited to tell Zoey and the rest of the world their good news. It had been a fun weekend spent in the safety of the hotel room in Sweden, telling each other everything about themselves and their pasts, down to which kind of toothpaste was their favorite.

"Actually, it wasn't too bad." Mindy smiled as she sat Anya on the porch and knelt down in front of her. "Before we go inside—Anya, I have a little surprise for you." She reached in her purse and pulled out a Barbie dressed in a bridal gown.

"Oh, she pretty." Anya took the doll and pulled it to her chest, smoothing the doll's hair like it was her own personal baby.

"Look, Anya." She motioned for her to more closely examine the doll's hand. "She has a ring on."

Anya nodded as she stared down at the doll's hand. "Anta?" she asked, confusion on her face.

"Look." Mindy stretched out her hand so both Zoey and Anya could see the diamond ring that Jarrod had bought her. "Jarrod gave me this."

Zoey squealed beside them, and she jumped from foot to foot and wrapped her arms around her brother's neck. "Yeah, you guys! I knew it!"

"Always the family planner." Jarrod laughed, giving her a quick peck on the cheek.

"But first," Jarrod said, turning back to the little one. "I have to ask… Do you think it would be okay if your auntie marries me?"

Anya toddled over to him. She wrapped her arms around his legs, the Barbie still in her hand, and looked up at him, giving him a wide smile and an enthusiastic nod.

He lifted her into his arms.

"Okay," Anya said, snuggling into his chest. She reached out for Mindy. "You're Anta." Then she pointed to herself. "I'm Anya."

"Yes, baby girl. I'm Anta and you're Anya."

"Uh-huh," Anya said, smoothing her doll's hair. "Anta and Anya. I just like you." She gave her a sweet smile. "I love you, Anta."

Mindy moved to them and wrapped Anya and Jarrod in her arms as tears filled her eyes. "I love you, too, little one."

Anya rested her cheek against hers. "And Jarrod?"

"Yes, baby girl, I love Jarrod, too." She smiled as Jarrod wrapped his arm around her and pulled her tighter into their new family's embrace.

"I love you, too, my girls," Jarrod said, looking over at his sister.

For once in her life, Mindy was at peace. At

least for now. The future, though she knew it would bring its own set of troubles and upheavals, looked bright. She would spend it with the people she truly loved, and she had no doubt that their lives would be nothing less than wonderful.

* * * * *

Look for Million Dollar Bounty
by Danica Winters,
the next book in the Stealth series,
available February 2020
wherever Harlequin Intrigue books
and ebooks are sold.

Get 4 FREE REWARDS!

We'll send you 2 FREE Books <u>plus</u> 2 FREE Mystery Gifts.

Harlequin Intrigue® books feature heroes and heroines that confront and survive danger while finding themselves irresistibly drawn to one another.

FREE Value Over $20

Love Harlequin romance?

DISCOVER.

Be the first to find out about promotions, news and exclusive content!

Facebook.com/HarlequinBooks

Twitter.com/HarlequinBooks

Instagram.com/HarlequinBooks

Pinterest.com/HarlequinBooks

ReaderService.com

EXPLORE.

Sign up for the Harlequin e-newsletter and download a free book from any series at **TryHarlequin.com.**

CONNECT.

Join our Harlequin community to share your thoughts and connect with other romance readers!
Facebook.com/groups/HarlequinConnection

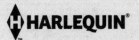

**ROMANCE WHEN
YOU NEED IT**

HSOCIAL2018